the GUARDIAN

L.M. Nelson

The Guardian
Copyright © 2018 L.M. Nelson

ISBN-13: 978-0-9985135-3-9

1 2 3 4 5 6 7 8 9 10

This is a work of fiction. The events and characters described herein are imaginary and are not intended to refer to specific places or living people.

Cover Design by Rachael Ritchey
All images in design used courtesy of CC0/public domain

Chapter 1

Reaching across the back seat, Camryn Hunter attempted to retrieve her cellphone by prying it out of her brother's hand. "If it's not yours then don't touch it!" she scolded him.

Toby held it behind his back. "If you want it, come and get it."

"Give it back!" she insisted, smacking her brother in the arm.

Clouds darkened the moonlit sky while the old car's windshield wipers slapped torrential rainwaters away. The headlights shone brightly down the backcountry mountain road, but there were no street lamps, no houses, and no other cars in sight; even the stars seemed to be hiding tonight.

Their father turned away from the road to reprimand his children. "Would you two stop arguing, please? Toby, get your own phone and give Camryn's back to her."

"The battery's dead on mine."

Camryn's mother released a blood-curdling scream. Quick to react, her father turned his eyes back to the road just in time to see a large shadow of a creature blocking their way. He slammed on the brakes. The tires squealed and the car spun out of control. Camryn echoed her mother's screams as the car began to roll, crashing into the blacktop with each turn. Her arm smashed against the side of the door, and shards of glass hit her in the face. The twirling, spinning motion made her dizzy. Then, with a sudden jolt, the car fell silent.

Camryn moaned, feeling disoriented. Still strapped in her seatbelt, her body hung limp. Pain resonated from her forehead. She reached up, checking for gashes and bumps, but found nothing.

Her younger brother moaned in the seat next to her. Hoping he wasn't injured, she called his name. "Toby?"

He groaned again.

"Are you ok? Are you hurt?"

"My elbow hurts."

She quickly scanned the vehicle. Her mother was hunched over the dashboard with her forehead flush against the windshield. "Mom?" Camryn called out, hoping to get a response. "Mom, are you ok?"

When her mother didn't answer, she fumbled around for her seatbelt and set herself free, falling to the ceiling with a thud. Once she regained her stability, she crawled over to the front passenger's seat and pulled her mother's body against the seat. Hoping to find signs of life, she felt for a pulse. Not even the faintest thump was felt.

Afraid to look, she turned to her father, whose lifeless body hung halfway out the broken driver's side window. "Daddy?"

From the back seat, Camryn's brother asked, "What's that smell?"

Camryn took a whiff. Gasoline. Panic-stricken, she climbed back to help Toby release his seatbelt. "We need to get out of here. Now!" She supported his body as best she could and drug him out the shattered back window.

Toby hit his arm on the door frame. "Ouch, Camryn! That hurts!" he wailed.

"Then help me. Push with your legs."

With his help, she directed him out the window. Once on solid ground, she supported her brother's limping body and led him away from the car. The rain poured onto them, and their clothes were soaked. Camryn could still smell gasoline, but because it was so dark outside, she really couldn't see what kind of condition the car was in or even navigate where they were.

"Are Mom and Dad ok?" Toby asked.

Camryn looked around, trying to figure out where they were. But with only the moonlight to guide her, she couldn't see much.

"Camryn!" Toby yelled trying to get her attention. "Are Mom and Dad..."

A tremendous explosion lit up the darkness, startling them both.

"No!" Toby lunged toward the engulfed vehicle. Camryn grabbed his arm and held him back, sheltering him with her body. He fought to break free, but it was too late. Flames consumed the overturned vehicle and black smoke spewed from the underbelly. Toby buried his head in Camryn's chest, and they both sobbed as they watched the car burn.

The temperature dropped rapidly, making them both shiver. If they didn't find shelter soon, they would surely freeze to death. By now, the rain had let up a bit, and the moon peeked out through the clouds, offering just enough light to guide them. Huddled together, they traversed through the wilderness seeking a safe haven that would provide them with protective shelter for the night.

Several yards into the woods, Camryn spotted what looked like a cave on the side of a hill. "Wait here," she said to her brother.

Toby didn't like this situation. Not only was he left alone in the dark, but he also feared that an angry animal might try to attack his sister. "Camryn," he muttered. "Come back here."

"Toby, I'm fine." She approached the rocky structure and peeked inside. The cave wasn't a huge sanctuary, but it was big enough and far enough out of the elements to house them for the night. "Come on," she encouraged him. "We'll be safe here."

Together, they entered the cave and made themselves as comfortable as possible.

Blood dripped from Toby's elbow. "You're bleeding," Camryn said to him. Hoping to get a better look at his injury, she turned his arm toward her. The skin on his elbow had been scraped away, leaving a three-inch gash that was red and swollen. "Let me wrap it for you."

She tore a long strip of fabric from the bottom of her shirt and did her best to wipe the blood away. With the cloth, she wrapped his elbow, tying it off with a knot to apply direct pressure, which would hopefully stop the bleeding. "Does that feel better?"

"Thank you." He pulled his elbow back. With tears streaming down his face, Toby leaned into Camryn. "What are we supposed to do now?"

"I don't know." She sat against the cave wall and snuggled in closer to her brother, putting her arm around him to keep him warm. "In the morning, when it's light out, we'll try to figure it out."

Rest did not come easily. Toby cried most of the night, and nightmares woke him several times. The cold, hard ground was not conducive to sleep, and the damp air of the cave left goose bumps on both his and Camryn's skin. Huddled together for warmth, Camryn kept watch over her younger sibling. She did her best to comfort him, but her own emotional state was far from stable. Her puffy eyes ached from the countless tears she'd shed, and images of her parents' faces filled her thoughts. Fear overtook her, and uncertainty flooded her mind. How were she and Toby going survive on their own?

Every muscle in Camryn's body ached. Yet somehow, with the rising of the sun, she mustered up the strength to stand on her own two feet.

Toby lay curled up in a fetal position on the ground next to her. His blood-soaked bandage was now dry, indication that the bleeding had diminished and his wound was healing. Reassured that her brother was alright, Camryn stepped out of the cave and took in a big breath of air. Her eyes widened, and she instantly lost her breath when a frightening sight met her eyes. "Toby!" she yelled, rousing him from his slumber. "Toby, wake up! Come out here quick!"

Toby rubbed his tired eyes and stepped out of the cave to join her. "What is your problem? Why'd you have to…" Then he saw why she had made such a fuss. "Where's the car?"

Camryn scanned the entire area but found no signs of wreckage, no debris, no indication at all that an accident had occurred here. "This can't be happening." She raised her hand to her forehead trying to make sense of the situation. There were no hints of civilization in this area, no cell towers indicating phone coverage, not even electrical wires or mile markers. It was pretty remote. The chances of anyone witnessing this accident were unlikely. Yet, the entire vehicle had gone missing, leaving no traces behind at all.

She stepped onto the road and stood beside a pine tree. "This doesn't make any sense. It can't just disappear." A metal barrier separated the asphalt from a large ravine, yet the car hadn't broken through it. The barrier was completely intact. She peeked over the edge, thinking she might find the car down there. Nothing but rocks.

Toby plopped on the ground near a boulder. Convinced they were both going to die here, he picked at the grass around him. Hidden within the blades, two shiny metal objects glistened in the sunlight. He rustled through the grass and dug out a pair of golden rings. He held them in his hand and stared at them. Each had unusual words engraved on the inside of the band in a language Toby didn't understand.

Camryn stepped away from the ravine and moved closer to her brother. "What are you looking at?"

He held out his hand to show her. "These."

"Where did you find those?"

"Right here in the grass."

She held one of the rings between her thumb and forefinger and examined it carefully. As she analyzed the detailed engraving on the gold band, the boulder next to Toby appeared to shapeshift. It was now shaped like an arrow pointing toward the ravine. Camryn blinked twice and shook her head. "That's weird. Was that rock pointing that direction a minute ago?"

Mocking his sister, Toby said, "Of course it was. Rocks don't move on their own."

"Are you sure?"

"I'm sure." He stared at the shiny ring in his hand for a minute or two. "I wonder where these came from?"

He slipped one on his finger and vanished into thin air.

"Toby?" Camryn searched the entire area but couldn't find her brother anywhere. She didn't think Toby's sick idea of a joke was even the slightest bit amusing. "Toby, this isn't funny. Where are you?" Staring at the gold ring in her hand, she contemplated the meaning of this. Toby was sitting right in front of her, until he put on the ring. Although unlikely, the evidence suggested one thing. "No way. That's impossible."

Not sure what to expect, she slowly slipped the other ring on her finger. Within seconds, she was transported right to Toby's side. All around her, pine trees clung to the walls of a gorge, bending their trunks upward, and their needles were a strange shade of metallic green. These trees grew among tiny cliff dwellings, each with a thatched roof and small round windows. The leaf-covered tree branches hung low enough to shelter the houses from the elements and protect them from unwanted visitors. Some of these trees appeared to have faces with bright blue glowing eyes and leafy fronds protruding from the top of their heads. Some of the older moss-covered trees had green vines wrapped around their trunks, stretching from the elongated facial features all the way down to the roots.

"What in the world?" Convinced they had stepped into some sort of Oz-like land similar to the one she had seen so many times in her favorite movie, Camryn's eyes focused on the details of the tree in front of her.

But Toby stood like a statue, gawking at the ravine with his mouth gaped open.

The cliff village busily buzzed with odd-looking, furry creatures. They were about three-feet high with green-toned skin and floppy jackrabbit-type ears. These creatures had long, skinny arms and legs with oversized toes, able to grasp tree limbs like tree frogs. They walked upright like humans did, but upon closer examination of one of these creatures, it appeared to have pixie wings. Several shrew-like rodents with monstrous feet and claws too big for their toes ran around the village making squeaking noises. They had fuzzy, striped tails, large eyes, and wore permanent smiles on their faces. When frightened, these creatures curled up like armadillos. Several brightly-colored tropical birds with multicolored plumes extending from the top of their heads flew around freely.

A beautiful large-winged Phoenix fished in the river that flowed through the center of the village. This river, in the brightest shade of blue, didn't meander like water naturally did. Instead, it ran perfectly straight with almost unflawed precision. Many giant beta fish with wispy tail appendages and large goldfish eyes happily jumped out of the water, acrobatically flipped in midair, then dove back in the river with a splash.

Alongside the riverbank stood several large trees with retractable suspension bridges attached to them. These bridges draped across the river, each connecting one side of the village to the other. Apparently this was their access across the water. The river itself fed into a small lagoon enclosed by a rock arch, which had a waterfall pouring down from all sides. The waterfall magically flowed from nowhere, and the water acted as a wall that blocked any entrance into or out of the village.

The aromatic scent of sweet-smelling blooms, the colorful array of tropical flowers, and the caws and joyful songs of the local birds added a touch of spark to the entire scene.

"Look at this place," Toby said, having never seen anything like this in the world he knew. "Where are we?"

"I don't know, but we are definitely not in Idaho anymore." Camryn stepped forward, awed by the mysteriousness of it all.

"Where are you going? Get back here," Toby insisted.

"I'm gonna go check it out. Come on."

Not feeling as adventurous as his sister, Toby didn't move.

Directing him to follow her, Camryn said, "Come on, Toby. Come with me." She trekked further down the trail toward the village.

Reluctantly, Toby ran after her.

Chapter 2

Camryn and Toby traversed down a small set of rock stairs that led to a pathway. As soon as their feet hit the path, the staircase behind them disappeared. Toby whined, "Great. Now we're trapped down here. How are we supposed to get out?"

"Where's your sense of adventure?" Camryn took his hand and led him down the path.

He jerked away from her. "No way. I am not taking another step. I'm getting out of here." Toby desperately searched for an exit. When he couldn't find one, he tugged at the ring on his finger and tried to pry it off his hand. It wouldn't budge.

"You're the one who put the ring on in the first place," Camryn reminded him.

"I didn't know it would lead us down here. How was I supposed to know that?"

As they debated, one of these odd, green, furry creatures stammered up the dirt-covered road and greeted them. "Welcome, my friends."

Camryn and Toby stopped dead in their tracks and gawked at the creature in front of them.

"We've been expecting you."

How could this odd-looking thing possibly be expecting them? There was no way this furry creature could have known that they were going to be stranded here after finding these gold rings that somehow transported them into this unusual land.

"Wait a minute," Camryn said. "You knew we were coming?"

"Of course." He extended a friendly bow. "You are the Guardian."

Camryn and Toby stared at each other. "The Guardian?"

The tiny creature reached out to Toby. "Come," he directed, encouraging Toby to follow him. "The great master awaits you."

Toby eyed Camryn, awaiting her advice. Camryn reassured him with a nod. Reluctantly, Toby trekked further down the path, tracing the creature's steps. Camryn trailed right behind them.

Entering the village, these creatures all bowed to them majestically. They were two kids from small town Idaho and certainly didn't hold a high status in society, yet these creatures favored them highly and treated them like royalty.

Toby leaned toward Camryn and whispered, "What are these creatures, and what do they want?"

She replied, "I don't know. Just keep walking."

As they hiked down the path, colorful flowers opened their pedals and reached their leaves out to Toby. Trees outstretched their branches, and watchful eyes of every living thing followed them, carefully examining Toby's every move. Hovering birds looked down on them, as if standing guard from high above. The entire village revered them.

The Guardian

The furry creature led Toby and Camryn across a suspension bridge to a gigantic Redwood tree in the center of the village. It was much larger than the surrounding trees. The branches drooped, and the outer bark was blanketed in thick, green moss. A wooden plank path encircled the tree and led to an open platform that stopped halfway up the trunk. They followed the furry creature to this platform where Toby now stood directly in front of the largest wood-carved face he had ever seen. The enormous nose, eyes, and mouth of this tree made Toby wish they hadn't ventured into this place. He stood as far away from the wrinkled face as he could.

The giant tree opened its large, blue eyes and lifted its head, making the platform quake. "Toby!"

The deep, ominous voice made Toby jump out of his skin. He took several steps back, stumbling over his own feet, and his face turned ghostly white. "You're a tree, a talking tree. How do you know my name? What do you want?"

"You are the discoverer of the great golden rings. You, and you alone, must open the gate."

Toby didn't like the way that sounded. "What gate?"

The tree raised its leaf-covered branch and pointed toward the waterfall at the far end of the village. "Venture out, beyond the great barrier."

Toby glanced that direction, wondering what lie beyond the river. "What's out there?"

"Beyond the forest, the enemy lies. Only the Guardian knows where he hides."

"What enemy?"

"The Firebeast fears he who holds the ring. The Guardian is his nemesis."

"Firebeast?" Toby questioned. "What's a Firebeast?"

"You must go," the tree demanded. "Seek he who threatens our land. Search for clues of his whereabouts. Find his weakness. Seek him out and destroy him. The ring will guide you along your path. Its power will give you the strength to defeat him." The tree closed its oversized eyes and fell silent, with its branch still pointing toward the waterfall.

"I can't defeat anyone. I'm just a kid from Idaho." Wanting no part of this, Toby again tried to pry the ring from his finger. He quickly realized it wasn't coming off. To make matters worse, the ring began to emit a bright, white light. Toby frantically turned his head from left to right, searching for a way out. "I'm not defeating anyone. I'm getting out of here."

"The only way out is through," the small, furry creature told him. "In order to return to whence you came, you must complete your quest. I shall gather provisions for your journey." The creature bowed to Toby then quickly departed.

Toby's voice trembled. "I can't defeat a Firebeast. I don't even know what a Firebeast is."

Trying to calm her brother, Camryn stated, "We'll figure it out. Quit acting like a baby."

"What are we supposed to do, Camryn?" He pointed to the waterfall. "We have no idea what's out there. Do you even know where we are? How will we know where to go? We have no guide, no weapons, no food, no water. We don't even have a working cellphone." He fell to the ground and buried his face in his hands. "We're going to die here."

"We are not going to die." Fighting her emotions, Camryn took a deep breath. "Didn't you hear what the tree said? He said the ring would guide you."

Toby looked down at the ring on his hand. How could a simple, gold ring possibly help them in this situation? "This is crazy, Camryn. I can't do this. I don't know how to fight. I'm afraid of spiders, and scary movies give me nightmares."

Placing her hands on his shoulders, she tried to help him focus. "I'll be with you the entire time. We'll get through this together, but we have to go forward."

Toby protested. "We don't know what's beyond that barrier."

"And we won't know if we don't go out there. For all we know, there may be an exit on the other side. I'm going out there to find out." She headed down the path toward the river. "Are you coming or not?"

Toby didn't want to die here. He didn't want to be left alone here either, so he followed Camryn down the path.

One of the creatures met them at the bottom. He had two satchels in his hand, one for each of them. "You have enough food and potable water for ten days. Ration wisely. Remember to use the ring's light to guide you."

Toby exhaled heavily. He didn't feel at all prepared for this.

Camryn put the satchel on her back and ventured into the water. "Come on, Toby."

Toby stared at his sister. He didn't want to do this, but knew Camryn wasn't backing down. Grudgingly, he slipped the satchel over his shoulders and followed her into the water.

As they crept closer to the waterfall, Toby saw no means to pass the barrier, yet the ring on his finger continued to glow. "How do we get through? Is there some sort of password or something?"

Camryn remembered what the tree druid told them. "Try the ring."

"I don't see what good that will do, but ok." Toby raised his fist and pointed the ring toward the waterfall. The ground trembled and a secret opening appeared in the center of the steady stream. Treading carefully, they squeezed their way through to the other side.

Chapter 3

A dark, eerie forest full of leafless trees showed signs of recent fire damage. Charred branches, blackened bark, and the smell of burning wood dominated this particular area.

Toby curled his lip. "It smells like burnt bacon." He touched a seared tree trunk, getting black soot on his finger.

The forest floor felt soft under their feet. Camryn bent down and grabbed a handful of soil. This wasn't ordinary soil. It was a soft, grey powder that easily slipped through her fingers and floated away in the breeze. She sprinkled it into the air and further examined their surroundings. Trees with ebony bark poked up from the ground like toothpicks. Stumps, singed and chiseled down to charcoal nubs, circled the area around them. Broken branches and uprooted trees created a maze of rubble. Scorched, discolored leaves crunched under their feet. Stones had been pounded away to dust, and large scratch marks covered every rocky surface. The only signs of life came from a strange vine with thick, two-inch thorns that clung to the side of an enormous boulder.

"What happened here?" Camryn reached out to touch the vine.

Toby pushed her hand away. "Why are you touching that?"

"Are you going to freak out about every little thing? Sheesh. It's just a plant."

"It might be poisonous," Toby warned. "Leave it alone."

Adhering Toby's advice, Camryn withdrew her hand.

Black clouds hovered overhead, and sheet lightning flashed across the sky. The roaring rumble of thunder shook the ground beneath their feet. Shadows lingered behind every tree, and glowing eyes watched them from every angle. Almost no light was visible, and strange, grumbling sounds lurked in the darkness. "I don't like this forest," Toby said. "It's dark and creepy."

A high canyon wall blocked their path on the left, but to the right, a single beam of light in the distance revealed colorful fronds and green wax-coated leaves. "The damage seems to be contained to this area," Camryn said. "It's not burned over there." She pointed that direction.

With a roaring rumble, the waterfall closed behind them, sealed by a stone wall.

"Great. Now what do we do?" Toby whined. "We can't go back now even if we want to."

"We press on." Camryn headed toward the light. "Let's go this way."

Toby hesitated for a moment before he ran to catch up with her.

As they inched toward the light, unusual symbols appeared on the tree trunks around them. Celtic in nature, these symbols ranged from crescents and interwoven circles to trefoil shapes and knotted branches. Words imprinted in an unknown script appeared on the ground. Camryn examined the strange inscriptions. "This doesn't look like any language I've ever seen before."

"What do you think it means?" Toby asked.

"I don't know."

An iridescent amethyst light emitted from a nearby stone. Toby's ring began to glow purple. "Uh, Camryn?"

Remembering what the gigantic talking tree had told them, she said, "The ring is trying to guide you. Follow the light."

The closer they got to the purple stone, the brighter Toby's ring shone, and it seemed to draw him in like a magnet. Only a few feet away from the stone, Camryn could see that the same words written on the ground were now written on this lodestone. "These symbols must be important. They're written all over the place."

"Kia-lekota raktas," a gravelly voice whispered from beyond the stone.

Toby's eyes fixated on the light, hypnotized by its radiance. He stepped closer, extending his hand toward the rock.

"Kia-lekota raktas," the voice said again, more eerily this time.

The lodestone trembled, causing cracks to emerge on the surface. The purple light became brighter, almost blinding. Camryn squinted and shaded her eyes with her hand. "Toby?"

A hole opened in the middle of the rock. Toby stepped forward, within inches of the purple stone. The opening grew larger and the light brighter, illuminating the entire forest.

"Toby!" Camryn yelled.

But Toby didn't hear her. He was drawn to the stone, moving closer and closer, as if sucked in by a vacuum.

The voice became louder. "Kia-lekota raktas!"

Toby couldn't pull his eyes away. Hypnotized, he reached his hand into the open chasm and chanted, "Kia-lekota raktas!"

Instantly the vacuum effect ceased, the light diminished, and the golden band on Toby's finger lost its glow. Toby withdrew his hand, sweating and panting profusely.

Camryn rushed to his side. "Are you ok?"

Trying to catch his breath, he said, "I saw this cave. This dark, musty cave. It was surrounded by sharp rocks and fiery flames. It pulled me in, and I couldn't escape. I…" The world around him began to spin. Feeling weak, he fell to his knees.

Camryn hugged him tightly. "It's okay. You're going to be okay."

A large, black skeleton key emerged from the rock opening. Toby picked it up and stared at it. "What is this?"

The same inscription that had been on the ground and the rock now appeared on this key, along with a bright orange gemstone. "Obviously these words mean something," Camryn said. "Until we find out what, we better hang onto this." She shoved the key in her bag and pulled out a flask of water. "Here. Drink this."

Toby swallowed several gulps to regain his strength. "What does kia-lekota raktas mean?"

"I don't know." Camryn stood up and held her hand out to Toby. "Come on. Let's keep moving."

Toby rose to his feet, and they continued down a moss-covered path.

The further into the forest they ventured, the darker and more unnerving it became. Black clouds swirled overhead. Crisp leaves blew around freely, and the trees along the path howled with the wind. The entire terrain was covered with pointy rocks and sharp-edged boulders. The musty smell of decaying leaves combined with the smell of burning wood made Toby gag.

"We've been walking for hours," he said, wishing he could sit in his living room and watch TV. "I'm tired."

They found an overturned log and stopped to rest. Camryn pulled the key from her satchel and stared at it, mesmerized. "I wonder what this is for?"

"It's a key, dummy. Obviously it unlocks something." Toby reached into his backpack and pulled out a flask. Right as he was about to take a drink, a deep growl emerged from the woods behind them. "I don't like that sound."

The growl turned into more of a whimper, as if an animal was in pain. Camryn listened more intently. The whimper came from a thicket only a few feet away. "It's coming from over here." She stood up and walked that direction.

"Are you crazy? How do you know that thing won't attack you?"

"You're such a baby. Quit being a scaredy cat." Ignoring her brother's concerns, she cautiously crept into the brush.

A grey wolf lay on the ground trying to gnaw its way free from a netted trap. When the wolf spotted Camryn, it snarled and drooled like a rabid dog.

She knelt down to its level. "It's alright. I'm not going to hurt you."

Toby ran into the thicket, searching for his sister. "Camryn, where are you?" When he saw the wolf, he froze. This wolf's head was large and lean, much bigger than a normal sized wolf. It had a more pronounced muzzle too, and its strong, muscular legs were longer in proportion to its body. Toby recognized this animal right away. "That's a dire wolf," he said.

The animal whined again.

Toby examined the wolf's features more critically. It had fierce eyes and steel-like fangs. Knowing this animal was dangerous, he tried to call his sister back. "Camryn, that thing has powerful jaws. It can and will rip you apart."

"But it's just a baby," Camryn argued, and she scooted closer. "He needs help." She allowed the wolf pup to sniff her hand, then she scratched it on the head to let it know she wasn't a threat.

Toby reached into his pocket and pulled out his pocketknife. He moved closer to the wolf and flipped the knife open.

Startled by this sudden motion, the wolf snarled at him, barring its teeth.

"Let him know that you're not here to hurt him," Camryn advised. "Let him take in your scent."

Cautiously, Toby reached his hand out to the wolf, who in turn sniffed his fingers and nudged at his hand.

"There you go, little guy." Camryn hoped her soothing voice would calm the beast. "We're here to help."

Toby carefully cut the ropes loose. As soon as the wolf was free, it darted back and licked its front paw then glared at Toby with glowing yellow eyes.

"He's staring me down," Toby's voice shook. "Why do I have a feeling I'm about to become his lunch?"

Camryn used her knowledge of canines to distract the wolf. She picked up a stick and waved it in the air. "Here, boy. Wanna play?"

With eyes focused solely on the wolf, Toby remarked, "It's not a puppy, Camryn. It's a menacing carnivore, and it wants to eat me."

"No he doesn't. He's just scared." Camryn sat on the ground in front of the wolf.

To Toby's surprise, the wolf reclined onto its tummy and crawled over to Camryn, stretching its body submissively. As Camryn extended her hand to pet the beast, the wolf rolled over, allowing her access to its underbelly. "He's gentle, Toby. Look." She rubbed the wolf's tummy.

Toby crept closer, trying not to frighten the animal. He slipped his knife back in his pocket and sat on the ground with Camryn. "Is it hurt?" he asked, reaching his hand out to touch the animal.

Camryn inspected the wolf's exterior, finding nothing but a bloody area on its leg. It yelped when she touched it. "Doesn't seem to be anything serious. His leg is obviously injured, though."

Toby untied the strip of fabric from his elbow and used it to wrap the animal's wound. "There you go. You'll heal up nicely now."

The wolf pup whimpered and nudged Toby's arm affectionately.

Toby grinned. "He's not ferocious at all."

"I think he's glad we rescued him. We probably saved his life."

They hung out with the pup while they rationed out food to satisfy their hunger. Toby even shared his rations with the wolf.

As the air began to chill and the moon's glow illuminated eerily over the treetops, Camryn and Toby grew weary. They found a clearing and decided to make camp for the night.

Toby gathered several thin sticks and branches, a few pinecones, dried moss and pine needles, and pieces of bark. He formed a circle with nearby rocks then shaped the dried moss and pine needles into a nest in the center. He laid pinecones and dried branches all around the tinder bed. Once he had everything set up, he carved an inch-thick fireboard and bore a small hole on the end with his pocketknife. When he was done, he picked up a branch and tapered the tip like a pencil. Using his shoelace, a rock, and a flexible branch, he built a bow and socket. He placed the fireboard on the ground and held it in place with his foot. He knelt on his knee, inserted his handmade drill into the fireboard, and began to saw back and forth, faster and faster, putting more pressure on the socket with each stroke. Eventually, black powder and smoke formed around the bottom of the drill. He gently fanned it with his hand until an ember formed. He placed the ember into the tinder bundle and gently blew until it caught fire. When a flame was established, he added toothpick-sized sticks, then pencil-sized branches, followed by increasingly bigger items, creating heat.

Toby had been camping in the woods hundreds of times and felt comfortable in the wilderness, but these woods were different. The noises were mysterious, shadows lurked everywhere, and every object appeared to be staring at them. "What are we going to do if we can't get out of here?" he asked his sister while he warmed himself by the fire.

With a crooked grin, Camryn replied, "I kinda like it here."

The Guardian

Toby whipped his head around. "Are you crazy? This place gives me the heevie-jeevies. The forest has eyes, the trees talk, and the rocks light up and chant in strange languages."

"That's what makes it cool. You tell me all the time that you wish our lives were more exciting. Well, it doesn't get much more exciting than this."

"I want excitement and adventure, but I don't want to die." The wolf pup, who hadn't left their side, positioned himself between the two of them and sat on his haunches keeping guard. Toby felt much safer having a wolf close by. "At least we have some sort of protection from the creepy things that live in this forest."

Camryn rolled her eyes. "What are you so afraid of?"

"We don't know what's out there, Camryn. How are we supposed to defeat a Firebeast? Did you see the size of the claw marks back by the waterfall? If those are the Firebeast's markings, we're as good as dead." Toby fluffed his jacket to make a pillow and reclined on the ground. "I miss Mom and Dad, and I want to go home."

"I miss them too. And I wish we could go home, but we can't. So until we find a way out of here, we need to make the best of this situation."

Toby grumbled under his breath. "How can we possibly make the best of anything when all we have are rocks and dirt and creatures in the forest who want to eat us?"

"We have each other, and right now we have to rely on that. We can't just give up. We have to press forward, whether you want to or not."

Chapter 4

Toby and Camryn slept warmly that night, guarded by the wolf. Yet their slumber was rudely interrupted when Toby's ring gave off a high-pitched humming sound. He opened his eyes to see it glowing luminously.

The wolf pup immediately sat up and growled deep within his throat.

Toby patted his side. "Easy, boy."

Camryn popped up and quickly scanned the surrounding area. "What is it?"

Toby shook his head. "I don't know." He stood on a nearby log to get a better vantage point, but it was so dark beyond their campsite, he couldn't see a thing.

The wolf's hackles spiked, and he crouched lower to the ground, ready to pounce on whatever was stalking them.

"What is it, boy? What do you see?"

A tiny wrinkled man with an elongated nose and long, pointy ears popped out from behind a tree. His tattered clothes, leather bracers, and animal hide boots blended well with the natural surroundings. Raising a wooden, stone-tipped staff, he said, "Put out that light. Are you trying to attract attention?" He kicked dirt over their fire, smothering the flames.

"Hey, stop that," Toby protested. "We need that fire for warmth and protection."

"Protection?" the little man said, waving his staff in the air. "These rocky woodlands hold you no harm."

Toby dug through the dirt for any embers he could salvage. As he did, the gold band on his finger shone brightly, emitting a light far brighter than the fire that had been doused.

"Ah," the little man said, honing in on the illuminated ring on Toby's finger. "You hold possession of the ring."

Toby stared at his hand. A spiral symbol appeared on the ring's surface, something he had never seen before. "Yeah. So?"

"That ring has great power."

"I don't know what you're talking about. It's just an old ring."

The old man explained, "Did it not lead you through the water barrier? Did it not direct you to the lodestone? Only the Guardian has the wisdom to control the ring's power. You would not be here now if not for the power within the ring."

Camryn openly laughed. "Wisdom. Toby can't even spell the word wisdom."

"Shut up!" he snapped at her. "I can so."

"What you seek does not lie in the depths of these woods. What you seek lies far beyond the tree line, where the elements converge. From there, you must venture into Alderwood."

"Alderwood?"

"Yes. Alderwood is a sacred forest where the Treelings once lived. The Treelings hold great power. They connect the forest with the elements, and they use this connection to maintain peace among the tribes and clans of Gelnoff.

The Guardian

Generations ago, the Firebeast discovered the power the Treelings had over the elements. Hoping to gain sole possession of that power, he bound the Treelings into slavery and starved them to near extinction. The only way to escape his tyranny and save their clan from total annihilation was to go into exile. No one has seen or heard from them for centuries. Since the Firebeast has been unable to locate them, he wreaks havoc on every village in Gelnoff, insistent that the inhabitants reveal the location of his former slaves. He seeks destruction to all who defy him. His wrath has greatly affected every being in Gelnoff. He burns villages, murders elders, and uses his domination to steal young ones and force them into servanthood. He has enslaved members of every clan to the east and west of the great divide. His greed and destruction has weakened the elements, disrupted the flow of nature, and destroyed the peace that held Gelnoff together for thousands of years."

Fascinated by this story, Camryn and Toby sat down to listen.

"Without the Treelings, the elements became disjointed. Farmlands became parched and festered with salt. Drinkable water turned noxious. Raging fires choked the trees, and the air became stagnant. Ancient legend has stated that a Guardian, a ring bearer, would put an end to this destruction and set the Treelings free. Once the Treelings reclaim Alderwood, the ancient forest will once again come alive, and the elements will regain strength. Only when the elements are harmonized will Gelnoff once again know peace. Only one has the insight and power to accomplish this—the one who holds possession of the ring."

Toby twirled the gold ring around his finger and examined the spiral engraving. "Why do all these weird words and pictures keep popping up all over the place? What do they mean?"

"The elements communicate with you through the ring. The symbols are messages, written to guide you. You have to use the elements to your advantage if you want to defeat the Firebeast." The old man reached into his knapsack and pulled out a leather-bound book with the same spiral symbol printed on the front. The whole thing was sealed by a locket. "Within the pages of this tome, the elements speak. These elements are inherently neutral, and neither is good nor bad, but each has its own distinct power. It's your responsibility to learn how to use that power."

Toby gripped the book in his hand.

"But you must use the powers wisely. Proper use of the elements can make you invincible. Misuse can lead to disaster. Good luck, Guardian." The wrinkled man bowed and vanished just as quickly as he appeared.

Toby stared at the sealed manuscript. "What am I supposed to do with this?"

Camryn pointed to the words on the front—*Elementis Libri*. "It's a book of elements." She took the book from him and carefully unlatched the locket. Every page revealed sketches of landscapes, diagrams, maps, and various chants, illustrated with Celtic symbols. "It's written in Latin."

"Can you read it?" Toby asked.

She flipped through the book and stopped on a page with a drawing of four rocks arranged in a circle, each with a different symbol carved onto it. "I think it says something about the sacred circle, but I'm not exactly sure. I'll look again in the morning when there's more light."

With the rising of the sun, Camryn, Toby, and the wolf continued their journey, searching for the ancient forest of

Alderwood. While they walked, Camryn skimmed through various pages of this sacred book and read the information out loud. "It says here that the Earth element provides endurance and strength. Air offers dexterity and acuity and provides wisdom of the mind. Fire gives courage, and Water has healing powers. But when all four elements are combined together, they create a sacred circle that invokes protection and…" When Camryn looked up, Toby wasn't behind her like she though he would be. She looked all around but didn't see him anywhere. "Toby, where are you?"

About thirty yards in front of her, she spotted him and the wolf pup in the middle of the path eyeing an unusual rock formation. She closed the book and walked toward them.

Four stones formed a large circle. To the north, the stone was engraved with three green circles enclosed within a box. To the east, a yellow triple spiral was etched on the stone. The southern stone had a single red flame carved onto it, and the stone to the west was marked with three blue, horizontal, wavy lines. On the ground, smack in the middle, were four outer circles connected by an inner circle.

"Whoa," Toby said, fascinated by the rocky structure. "What is this?"

Camryn flipped through the tome to search for clues. She stopped when she came to a drawing of these five interconnected circles. "It says here that the four outer circles symbolize the four elements. The middle circle unites them all, bringing balance to their energies." That's when she recalled the conversation they had with the wrinkled man. "Remember what the old man said? He said that we had to go beyond the tree line, where the elements converge. This must be what he was talking about."

This circle of stones was positioned right next to a riverbank. The wolf pup leaned over to take a drink while Toby pulled out his flask and dipped it into the water. A glint of light caught his eye. He turned his head toward the light and spotted something shiny sparkling under the water's surface. He set the flask on the ground next to him and reached his hand further into the shallow river.

Camryn tried to stop him. "What are you doing?"

"There's something down there."

"Leave it alone. We need to keep moving."

But Toby didn't listen to her. He gripped the sparkling object and pulled it out of the water. His ring glowed bright green, along with the sword in his hand. "Cool," he said, examining the intricate details. Interconnected circles were engraved on the pommel with a crisscross design etched into the strong, steel grip. The crossguard was decorated with sparkly green gems, and a lion's head poked out on both sides. Engraved on the base of the blade was the same circular pattern that appeared in the center of the rock formation. Toby marveled at the prize he had found. "Camryn, check this out."

"Put that down."

Again, he ignored her request. Instead, he tied a piece of fabric around his waist to hold the sword securely against his body.

"What are you going to do with that? You don't know how to use a sword."

"So?"

"So, you're going to hurt yourself."

"No I'm not." With his flask now full, he took a quick gulp and shoved it back in his bag. "Which way should we go?"

Camryn pivoted her body toward an arched, moss-covered, medieval stone bridge that stretched across the river. "I say we go that way."

Toby agreed that was a good idea.

On the other side of the bridge, the landscape drastically changed. Grass covered every inch of the forest, and ferns and wildflowers lined the path. Majestic trees, over a hundred feet tall, created a tunnel that shaded an otherwise sunny path. The gaps between the droopy branches allowed light to shine through. The trees, with their white, feathery leaves, dropped soft white petals onto the ground.

"This is much better than that creepy forest we were in," Toby said, wiping a flower petal off his arm. "And it doesn't smell like a cesspool."

Camryn took in a big whiff of air. The entire area was filled with flowering fields and smelled of fresh blossoms. "The scenery is certainly a lot nicer, and these flowers are beautiful. They remind me of Mom."

She bent over to sniff a blue bell-shaped flower when a man with leaf covered arms and mossy hair popped his head out of the tall grass. Camryn stumbled backwards and fell on her butt.

The wolf chuffed, and Toby pulled out his sword and pointed it at the strange creature. "Back off, bushman."

Startled, the creature held up his thin, wooden arms. "Drop your weapon. I mean you no harm."

Camryn rose to her feet and dusted dirt off her pants. "Put that sword away, Toby. You're going to kill someone."

Toby returned the sword to his waist and sneered at this odd-looking creature. "Who or what is that thing?"

The creature bowed. "I am Tyree, druid of Alderwood, the ancient forest of Gelnoff." The druid stepped out of the grass and joined Toby and Camryn on the path. "Why have you come here?"

"Some old, wrinkled dude told us to."

The druid curiously eyed Toby's sword. "That weapon you carry. Where did you get it?"

Toby glanced over his shoulder. "I pulled it out of that creek back there."

"That is the sword of Aonghus."

Toby looked the druid straight in the eye. "The what?"

"The sword of Aonghus. That sword was forged by an ancient clan of tree dwellers. They were masters of the elements. He who holds the sword has the power to bind the elements in various proportions."

Toby placed his hand on the pommel of the sword. "The Treelings made this?"

The druid took a step back. "You know of the Treelings?"

"Yeah," Toby replied, nonchalantly. "The old guy told us about them."

When Camryn reached into her bag to grab her water flask, the druid spotted the leather-bound tome. "You possess the book of elements too," he said with his jaw gaped open.

Camryn looked up. "The old man in the forest gave it to us. He said the elements speak through this book."

"They do, but the elements must communicate and work together as one or balance is disrupted. The Treelings knew this, and they knew how to create balance among the elements, which is why they were held in such high esteem in these lands. In his pursuit to gain control, the Firebeast has taken this balance away from us. He's disrupted the elements and caused great disharmony. The only way to bring balance back to Gelnoff is to stop the Firebeast."

"I know, I know," Toby complained. "And for some stupid reason, I've been chosen to do that."

"Yes. You possess the sword of Aonghus. You are the only one who can."

"And how, exactly, am I supposed to do that?"

"Look at the trees around you. The elements reside within them. The roots absorb water and minerals from the earth, and the leaves breathe in air and receive light from the sunbeams. If you set a tree on fire, the elements release from it. The oxygen the tree has been exhaling will enable the burning process. The water will evaporate, the light that has shone on the tree for many long years will burn out, and the nutrients from the soil will turn to ash, which will serve as a mineral source for other lifeforms. Without all four elements, the trees cannot grow. The trees are our life force, and the trees exist because of the elements. The elements create balance."

With furrowed brows, Toby gazed at a tree and rubbed his chin. "So I need to burn down all the trees to release the elements?"

"No. You need to channel the power within them."

"How?"

"I do not know. To find the answers you seek, into the ruins you must sneak."

Toby paced around in a circle. "How come no one around here ever answers my questions? Instead you throw a book at me that I don't understand, carve symbols into rocks that don't make sense, and speak to me in rhymes and riddles. Why should I care about bringing balance back to Gelnoff? What if I choose not to defeat this Firebeast? Why isn't anyone asking me what I want?" He gripped the sword in his hand and pointed the blade at the druid. "Get away from me, you creepy bushman. I'm finding a way out of here."

"The only way out is through."

Toby had heard that line before and didn't want to hear it again. "Ugh. I hate this place." He raised his hand to his forehead and sat on a nearby stump. "I'm hungry, I'm tired, and I want to go home."

Camryn tried to calm him. "It's gonna be ok."

"No, it's not ok, Camryn. Our parents are dead, we're trapped in this dumb forest land, and everyone in this place is crazy. We're never going to get out of here alive."

"Yes we will. We just have to keep pressing forward."

Toby stood up and glared at her. "You're as stupid as this bushman." He turned away and stormed off down the path.

Camryn shook her head and sighed. "You'll have to forgive my brother. He tends to open his mouth before he thinks things through."

"He is young and needs guidance," the druid stated. "But guidance cannot be had if he is not a willing recipient. You are wise for your years, and I sense you care for him deeply."

"I do."

"Then watch over him. Keep him safe."

With a nod, Camryn said, "I will."

Chapter 5

Further into Alderwood, the woodland garden became thicker. More wildflowers appeared in various shades of purple, yellow, and blue. Wisteria trees hung their fragrant blossoms over the footpath. Large-leafed plants, wispy ferns, and tall grasses covered every inch of the forest floor.

As Camryn and Toby hiked down the path, the sound of cracking sticks lingered in the trees. The dire wolf turned his head and growled at the noise.

"Who's there?" Toby grabbed his sword and stood behind the wolf in attack position, ready to strike whatever popped out of the foliage.

A large human figure with a bull's head crept out of the thick vegetation. This huge beast, probably ten feet tall, had biceps the size of Toby's head. He carried a double-bladed battleax, wore a loin cloth, and had armored plates all over the core of his body. His strong arms were covered in chainmail and the holes on his helmet allowed his horns to poke through. Toby drew his sword and charged toward the armored beast, swinging violently.

The beast huffed then gripped the sword and twisted it behind Toby's back. "You dare to attack me?"

Toby winced, and the strength of the creature's hands forced him to drop his weapon.

The creature laughed at Toby's lack of skill. "Why do you possess a weapon you do not know how to use?"

"Let go of me." Toby squirmed and tried to wiggle free, but the beast was too strong.

"You are dangerously close to Minotaur territory," the creature warned. "And we do not welcome unwanted guests. What are you doing in this part of the forest?"

"We're trying to get to the ruins."

"Why?"

"The druid of Alderwood sent us."

The Minotaur fixated on Toby's sword. "I've seen that sword before. Where did you get it?"

"I pulled it out of the river."

"The river allowed you to remove it?"

"Yeah. What's the big deal?"

The Minotaur released his grip on Toby. "You are the Guardian."

"So I've been told."

The dire wolf eased from attack stance and lay down in the grass. Sensing that the wolf no longer felt threatened, Toby also withdrew. He flexed his hand a few times to loosen the tension then straightened his shirttail.

"Please accept my apologies. I did not know who you were." The Minotaur took off his helmet and knelt down on one knee. "I am Noraz, gatekeeper of the labyrinth."

The Minotaur's face was scarred, and his arms and legs were battered and bruised. "What happened to you?" Toby asked, then he picked up his sword and leaned it against a nearby tree.

"Battle wounds." The Minotaur gave a derisive snort and limped over to the edge of the path. "Years of unrest and fighting to protect what's left of my home."

"Do you live in this forest?"

"I protect the ancient labyrinth on the edge of Alderwood where my clan once lived. The Minotaurs once claimed the dark forests of Gelnoff and controlled passage through the labyrinth. Now, I am the only one who remains."

"Why?"

"The Firebeast has long tormented this land, torturing clan members and forcing them into hiding. Even with the threat of capture and enslavement, my family and I chose to stay behind to protect the labyrinth. When the Firebeast learned that the Minotaurs had fled, he tortured my wife and forced her to reveal the clan's whereabouts. She refused to tell him. In a fit of rage, he killed her and kidnapped my children."

Toby's shoulders grew tense. "This Firebeast doesn't sound very friendly."

"The Firebeast will do anything he can to gain power over the elements and ultimately rule Gelnoff. He wants control, and I want revenge. Yet, I cannot defeat him. Only the Guardian has the power to stop him and end his path of destruction."

Toby took several steps backward. "I can't take on a Firebeast, and I don't want to. Look at me." Toby held out his arms, exposing his scrawny body. "Do I look like the kind of guy who can defeat a monster?"

The Minotaur huffed at Toby's feebleness. "Brute strength is not necessary. All that's needed is endurance, strong will, and intelligent use of the elements. You have a fighting spirit, and you have access to knowledge. You need to mentally prepare yourself for this task." The Minotaur picked up Toby's sword and handed it to him. "And if you're going to carry this weapon, you need to learn how to use it. We must begin your training."

Camryn followed the Minotaur down the path. As she walked past Toby, she shot him a probing glance. "Are you coming?"

Toby sat for a moment, wallowing in his own self-pity, before he strapped the sword to his side and followed them.

They walked for what seemed like hours. The entire time, Toby lagged behind, dragging his feet and thinking about his imminent death. If a ten-foot Minotaur couldn't defeat the Firebeast, how was he supposed to do it? He didn't know the first thing about fighting or swordsmanship. He didn't even know what a Firebeast was, let alone how to kill one. The more he thought about all of this, the gloomier he became.

At the far end of the path, a giant hedge blocked their way. "Wait here," the Minotaur said, then he stepped around the back of the bush.

Toby sat on the ground against a tree. He bent his knees, clasped his hands in his lap, and rested his chin on his knuckles. "I can't believe we got dragged into this. You don't act like you're the least bit concerned."

Camryn took a seat next to him. "I know this is not the most ideal situation, but we have more of a chance of surviving if we keep moving then we will if we just sit around and wait to be rescued. And you have to admit, this adventure is exciting."

"For you maybe. For me, moving forward brings us one step closer to danger. From what I've heard, this beast I'm supposed to defeat sounds like it can easily crush me. I'm heading to my death, and you don't seem to care."

"I care. But I think you're making assumptions. Everyone here seems to believe you can do this. Apparently they know something we haven't discovered yet." She pulled the book of elements out of her bag. "I think we need to read this more thoroughly. There's something in here we're missing."

The Minotaur returned with a suit of armor in his hand. He handed it to Toby. "Take this. At sunrise, we'll begin preparations and travel to the training grounds. In the meantime, you will need rest and nourishment. Come inside. I'll provide you with shelter."

Camryn and Toby gathered their belongings and followed the Minotaur behind the hedge into a complex branching maze system.

"This is the labyrinth of Moria," Noraz said. "Home of the Minotaur. Stay close. If trapped inside, you may never find your way out."

This giant maze had two stories of intricate stone passageways, most of which were underground and lit by endless torchlight. Each story contained thousands of rooms. They traveled up and down stairs, through corridors, into galleries, and in and out of various chambers before they entered a huge courtyard. The endless twists and turns of this complex tunnel system left them a bit disoriented.

"Where are we?" Toby asked.

"Underneath the ruins of Moria," the Minotaur replied. "Moria is the ancient city of Gelnoff. It was once occupied by the Aradatha tribe. The city used to be vibrant and lively. It flourished with colorful flowers, children playing in the streets, and tribesmen telling tales by firelight. But now, since the Aradatha have fled, the city is in ruins."

Toby raised his eyebrows. "When the druid told us about the ruins, he was talking about Moria, wasn't he?"

"Highly probable. But I don't know why he sent you this way. The ruins have been deserted for centuries." The Minotaur slapped a giant animal corpse onto a stone platform, raised his battleax above his head, and cleanly decapitated the corpse. The animal's head fell to the ground.

Its lifeless eyes stared at Camryn, making her stomach turn. "That is the most disgusting thing I have ever seen."

"A hearty meal is hard to come by these days. We must make do with what we have." The Minotaur ripped a slab of meat off the corpse and tore it apart with his teeth. He tossed a bone to the wolf then cut two steak-sized pieces and gave them to Toby and Camryn. "You must eat. We have a long journey ahead."

They cooked their meat on a skewer over an open flame while the wolf gnawed on his bone. Camryn flipped through pages of the tome searching for clues that might help them. She found a map with several landmarks, a page full of symbols she couldn't comprehend, and a list describing the powers of each element.

"Earth is nurturing and stable, full of endurance and strength. It is the element most deeply bound to the body. Earth binds Fire, Water, and Air in various proportions. Air is connected to the soul and the breath of life. It is a mental element, associated with knowledge and thoughtfulness. Air is the most versatile of elements, the most logical and efficient. It enables co-existence of the two main elements, Water and Fire. Fire is purifying and connected to strong will and energy. Fire can bring about new life or destroy the old and worn. It is the element of energy. Fire requires activity, vigorousness, and enthusiasm. However, it is unpredictable. Water is used for healing, cleansing, and purification and is associated with passion and emotion. When confronted with an obstacle, Water will split into rivulets and go around it, avoiding obstruction. It nurtures and sustains, yet is sometimes unstable." She scanned through various sections of the book hoping to find a magic spell, chant, or any other clue that might tell them how to capture the power of each element. "It doesn't say anything in here about how to use the elements. How do we know which ones to use, and how do we extract their powers?"

The Minotaur pulled out a leather pouch, tied closed with a leather strap. "Perhaps this will help."

"What is that?"

He untied the pouch and dumped a shiny, green stone about the size of a marble onto the table in front of them. "I found this near the river about the same time the Treelings went into exile."

Camryn flipped through the book again until she found a section titled *Statuas*. This page had a sketch of four small stones: green, blue, yellow, and red. Green represented Earth, blue denoted Water, yellow was Air, and red signified Fire. Each was labeled with the same symbols they saw earlier on the rock formation by the river. "It says here that a set of sacred stones was hidden within the borders of Gelnoff. Each stone holds an element's power. Only through proper channeling can the full power of the elements be unleashed." She looked over at the colorful stone on the table. "Is it possible that this is one of the sacred stones?"

"Hmmpf," Noraz snorted. "If it is, the Firebeast must not know of its existence."

Camryn read a detailed description. "Although each element is embodied in these stones, none holds power without the presence of the others. Only in combination do they reach their full capacity. If combined correctly, the elements' maximum energy is unleashed. If their powers are used erroneously, the elements become unstable."

"What is that supposed to mean?" Toby asked.

"I don't know, but according to this book, combining the elements is key to unleashing their power. Earth combined with Air creates great thoughtfulness. Air and Fire are powerful and logical. Air and Water generate adaptability. Earth and Fire produce sheer strength and unyielding patience. Earth and Water create deep-felt emotion. And Fire and Water have a general inclination to blast through any problem. The elements can also be combined in threes. Together, Earth, Air, and Fire are a strong force in both the rational and the physical. Earth, Water, and Air produce a sound grounding in reality and rational instinct. Earth, Water, and Fire are tenacious and undaunted. However, Fire, Air, and Water lead to loss of control and should be used with caution. But when all four elements are combined, they offer protective qualities. Anyone in the vicinity who is mentally strong enough will have undaunted ability to truly act. Energy will rage, sheer strength will surge, and unwavering courage will flow."

Toby held the bright green stone in his hand and stared at it. "How can a tiny rock do all that?"

"It's not the rocks that do it. It's the elements within the rocks, and learning how to channel and control their energy releases their power."

The Minotaur closed Toby's hand, hiding the stone from view. "You must keep this hidden. If word gets out that you possess one of the sacred stones, the Firebeast will surely find a way to acquire it from you. He knows of the stones' powers, but does not know how to control them. You, on the other hand, have the ability to channel the energy within them. Until you learn control, the stones are unstable."

"Where are the rest of the stones?"

"I do not know."

"Do you know how to channel their energy?"

"I do not. But a sage named Erramus knows the legend of the sacred stones. She might have some insights into the whereabouts of the others." Noraz leaned back and crossed his ankles. "Get some rest. In the morning, we will travel north to the training grounds."

Toby was awakened by a loud and terrifying roar. He stumbled backwards on the ground and bumped into a wall.

The Minotaur yawned, groaning as he stretched.

Toby held his hand over his pounding heart. "You scared the bejesus out of me." He quickly scanned the room for his sister, but Camryn was nowhere in sight. However, her backpack was on the floor along with her jacket. "What happened to my sister?"

The Minotaur grinned and licked his chops.

Beads of sweat formed over Toby's brow. He tightened his lips and tried to grip the wall behind him. "You ate my sister! Is that why you led us down here, so you could make a meal out of us?"

Noraz's deep laugh echoed through the tunnels. "Your lack of faith amuses me. If I planned to make a meal out of you, I would have done so last night." He slipped his chest plate over his shoulders and fastened it on the sides. "Your sister is in the next room, in the cleansing pool."

"There's a pool?"

"A cave pool. Take a moment to refresh, then we must be on our way."

Toby ran through a tunnel to the next room. This chamber was full of natural rock formations. Long, thin stalactites hung from the ceiling, and thick stalagmites poked up from the cave floor. A natural stream of water dripped into the pool, and the water was crystal clear.

"Toby, look at this," Camryn's voice bounced off the walls. "Isn't it fabulous?"

"Don't run off like that. I thought you were dead."

"I wanted to take a bath, so Noraz showed me this place." She swam to the edge and crawled out of the pool, dripping water all over the rocks. She wiped water from her face then stood next to Toby and cringed. "You should bathe too. You smell."

As Camryn exited the chamber, Toby sniffed his armpits. He turned his nose away from his own pungent odor then kicked off his shoes and took a dip in the pool.

While Toby dried himself and stepped back into his clothes, the Minotaur packed dried meat, a water flask, snares, and a box of first aid supplies into a pack. When the pack was full of necessary provisions, he placed the handle of a hatchet in the Molly strap, stuffed a dagger into a leather sheath, and snapped on a pair of bracers. He picked up a shield and clipped the cinch straps around the handle, holding it in place. When it was tightly secured, he belted his scabbard to his side and sheathed his sword. He threw the pack over his shoulder and picked up his battleax. "We must go. Grab your gear."

Toby slid his shirt over his head and tied his sword around his waist with a piece of cloth.

The Minotaur laughed at this sad excuse for a belt. "You need proper attire." He dug through a wooden chest and pulled out a leather scabbard and belt. "Use this."

The Guardian

Toby strapped on the belt then slid his sword into the sheath.

When he tried to fasten armor around his chest, the Minotaur snorted and shook his head. "Do not put that on yet. The excess weight will wear you down." Noraz threw a rope to him. "Attach your armor to your bag and carry it."

The Minotaur helped Toby tie his armor to his pack then they made a stop at the water well to fill their flasks before they meandered through the labyrinth's endless hallways.

Chapter 6

A light at the end of a tunnel led them to the opposite end of the maze. The landscape on this side of the labyrinth was dry and dusty. The wind blew red sand every direction, and eroded cliffs formed unusual rock formations. Acacia trees, junipers, and desert willows took refuge here, and the entire area was covered in sagebrush, needlegrass, and bright yellow bristlebush.

They followed a dirt-covered trail to the north. Sharp rocks lined the path, and tall grasses swayed in the wind. The steep, rocky terrain made walking more difficult, and the dry heat left Toby parched. He tried to swallow, but he had no saliva left in his throat. "I am so thirsty," he complained.

"Ration your water supply," Noraz advised. "Potable water is hard to find around here. Drink only when absolutely necessary."

Toby's mouth felt like it was full of cotton. He couldn't stand it any longer. He pulled his flask from his bag, unscrewed the lid, and chugged down over half the contents.

The Minotaur snatched the flask from his hand. "I said ration, you fool! That water must last until we reach another drinkable source."

"Why am I listening to you, you cow-faced…"

Before Toby could utter another word, the Minotaur shoved him against a tree and growled, "Do you want to die in this barren wasteland?"

With the Minotaur's hand wrapped tightly around his neck, Toby could barely breathe. He gasped for air and tried to pry himself free.

The Minotaur released his grip.

Once free, Toby fell to his knees and struggled to catch his breath.

Noraz sneered at him and dipped his eyebrows, giving him a glassy stare. "Foolish boy. Get up."

Toby rose to his feet and dusted sand off his pants.

"If you want to survive, I suggest you take a lesson in humility." The Minotaur shoved Toby's flask back into his bag and huffed derisively before he continued down the path.

As the sun began to set, the temperature drastically dropped. Seeking shelter, they stopped to rest under an acacia tree. Several feet away, they cleared a flat area and gathered kindling. Toby made a tinder bed with dried grass and sticks then Noraz pulled out a flint stone. Scraping the stone with his dagger, he created sparks, which hit the tinder and ignited. Toby gradually added small twigs until a decent-sized flame formed.

Noraz removed his armor and weapons and set them aside. Then he dug through his rucksack and retrieved a bag of dried meat. He broke off three pieces, one for Camryn, one for Toby, and one for the wolf pup. He ripped off a chunk for himself and removed the lid from his water flask to take a drink. "Rest. Tomorrow we will arrive at the training grounds." He leaned against the tree, gazed up at the stars, and chomped on his dried meat.

Trying to keep warm, Camryn and Toby scooted closer to the fire. The wolf pup rested by their feet. Wind whistled around them and an eerie aura filled the air. It gave Toby chills. "I have a bad feeling about this, Camryn."

"About what?"

"Being alone in this desert."

"We're not alone. We have a wolf and a Minotaur with us."

Toby shook his head. "That's not very reassuring."

"I think it is. Noraz is familiar with this area, and he knows how to survive in the wilderness. We need him on our side."

"I am aware of that."

"Then why are you constantly fighting him?" Camryn asked. "He's the only help we have right now, but with your attitude and the way you constantly defy him, I wouldn't be surprised if we woke up in the morning and found him gone. You need to listen to him or we're never going to get out of here."

Lying on the ground in a pile of sand and rocks didn't lend itself to a good night's sleep. Neither did the weird desert sounds. Toby awoke stiff and sore, and he didn't feel rested. He sat up and stretched then cast an eye over his environment. The dire wolf was curled up on the ground next to him, and the Minotaur was cooking something over a fire while engaged in conversation with Camryn.

Seeing that Toby was more or less alert, Noraz said, "Oh good. You're awake. We've made breakfast. Why don't you come join us?"

Toby rose to his feet.

"I found some fruit," Camryn said, and she handed her brother a handful of soft, red fruits.

Toby stared at them. "Are these edible?"

"Yes," Noraz replied. "Those are dates. They grow quite readily here."

He popped one in his mouth and savored its sweet flesh while he watched the Minotaur flip over a chunk of meat. "What is that?"

"Noraz killed a snake!"

Camryn was far too excited about this, but the thought of eating snake made Toby cringe. "Snake?"

"Yes." The Minotaur scraped a chunk onto an aluminum plate and handed it to Toby. "It's full of protein. Eat."

Reluctant at first, Toby pinched a small piece between his fingers and popped it in his mouth. It was a little chewy, but it didn't taste bad.

"We head out in thirty minutes," Noraz said. "Once we arrive, we'll restock supplies, make camp, and begin your training."

Toby mumbled under his breath, "Training for what? Why can't we just…"

Noraz instantly drew his dagger and held the blade at Toby's throat.

Toby gulped, but didn't move. He was afraid to move. If he did, the blade would surely slit his throat.

"A sword is a lethal weapon, and a sword fight is often decided in less than thirty seconds. You can't just wildly hit or bash at your opponent. You have to train if you want to stay alive. In combat, doing something wrong will get you killed. There are no shortcuts, and there is no middle-ground. I've trained in close quarters combat for hundreds of years. I've handled more kinds of weapons and swords than you can possibly imagine. It takes discipline and muscle memory to master each one. A sword can save your life, but it does you no good hanging in its sheath." The Minotaur huffed and returned his dagger to its scabbard. "The sooner we get to the training grounds, the better."

Toby brought his hand to his throat, checking for gashes. His body wasn't damaged, but his pride sure was.

When the Minotaur left to gather supplies, Camryn gave her brother a serious stare down. "That was a stupid thing to say. He's trying to help us."

Toby didn't agree. "He's trying to kill us."

"If he wanted us dead, he would have done it already. The poor guy has lost his entire family. Who knows how long he's been wandering alone in this wilderness. I think he genuinely wants to help us, and he seems to know what he's talking about, Toby. I would listen to him if I were you."

After breakfast, they headed further north. The farther up the trail they traveled, the less vegetation grew. Agave cactus, desert grass, and the occasional Joshua tree made its appearance, but overall, the landscape was dry and rocky. Buttes and jagged mountains rose from the horizon, and in the middle of the road, one lone rock structure stood on its end. It was etched with the same circular design as the river rock formation and the sword of Aonghus.

"There's that symbol again," Camryn said. "What does it mean?"

"The merging of the elements." Noraz hiked off the trail a few feet to the base of a butte. A pile of wind-sculpted sandstone boulders covered the ground around him. "This is where we stop."

Toby didn't see the point. There was nothing here except sand, a few tufts of desert grass, and some lizards. "We're in the middle of nowhere."

The Minotaur used his body weight to push a large boulder aside, creating an opening just wide enough to allow them access inside the butte. They squeezed through the opening, and Noraz returned the stone barrier to its proper place.

Inside was an abandoned encampment with several small huts, a large open courtyard, and a few acacia trees. A pair of archery targets, wooden scrap armor dummies, and a weapon rack full of embossed shields occupied a good portion of the interior courtyard. Piles of wood and rectangular plots where crops once grew surrounded the perimeter. A fire pit and water well stood in the center of it all. Although no one lived here now, it appeared that this area had once thrived with mighty warriors training for battle.

"Whoa," Toby said, fascinated by it all. "What is this place?"

"Welcome to the training grounds." Noraz set his pack on the ground and pulled a bucket from the well. "What's left of the water is fit to drink. Fill your flasks."

Both Toby and Camryn dunked their flasks into the water then each took a gulp to rehydrate.

"We'll have access to shelter, food, and water here. Choose a hut and rest a while."

These huts were surprisingly comfortable. Each had a wooden rope bed, quilted bedding, soft downy pillows, and a mattress stuffed with wool and straw. Each also had a small bedside table with an oil lamp, a chest to store belongings, and a washtub for personal grooming. A window with wooden shutters allowed natural light into the room. It wasn't home, but it was the closest thing they had to it for now.

Once Toby claimed his spot, he explored the encampment. One of the larger huts near the center of the village was built with strong stones and a thick oak door held together by metal rivets. Curious about this building, Toby crept closer. When he pushed open the door, the hinges creaked. Upon entering the hut, he discovered a rectangular table surrounded by long wooden benches that extended from one end of the table to the other. It looked like some kind of gathering area, perhaps for meals or to discuss battle plans. A circular iron chandelier with white candles for light dangled from the ceiling above. Several coats of arms decorated the archway entrance. At the far end of the room, a breastplate with two intersecting swords poking through it hung above a stone fireplace. Next to that, a long, intricately detailed bench stretched across the wall. Tucked neatly in a corner was an empty weapon rack. In the opposite corner, a large wooden trunk sealed by a brass hasp captured Toby's attention. Fascinated by the relic, he reached for the lid.

"Do not touch that," Noraz said from just inside the entrance.

"What's in it?"

"Nothing you need to be concerned about."

Ignoring the Minotaur's request, Toby lifted the lid.

Noraz slammed it closed, pounding the trunk with his fist. "Why must you be so meddlesome?"

"Why won't you let me see what's inside?" Toby countered.

"Snooping around will get you into trouble. You need to focus on the task at hand." He sealed the hasp with a nearby padlock.

Toby grumbled, "There's nothing fun to do around here."

"Fun?" The Minotaur's eyes widened. "This is not a game, boy. You were chosen to perform a very important task. You must take it seriously. I will do my part to help you, but we will accomplish nothing with your stubborn, reckless impatience. You see nothing beyond the here and now, and think of no one but yourself. We are here to prepare you for the task at hand. We don't have time for fun and games." With flaring nostrils, the Minotaur directed Toby toward the door. "At sunrise, we'll begin your training."

Toby dragged his feet toward the exit, followed by Noraz, who closed the door on his way out.

Finally able to rest comfortably, Toby slept better that night than he had in days. His peaceful slumber was rudely interrupted, however, when a deep, raspy voice called out, "Grab your sword and follow me." Ignoring the request, he buried his face under the covers.

Frustrated by Toby's lack of initiative, the Minotaur yanked the quilt off the bed and threw it on the floor. "We have much to do. We must get started." He threw open the shutters and allowed the early morning light to brighten the room.

The intense glare nearly blinded Toby. "Do you have to do that?"

"Yes. Get up. After a hearty meal, we will begin your first lesson."

Not feeling at all ambitious, Toby rolled out of bed. With the sun shining right in his face, he squinted his eyes to block the light. In the middle of the courtyard, the wolf pup ran around chasing bugs while Camryn held a wooden bow in her hands, attempting to shoot an arrow at a target. Her aim wasn't that accurate, but her form was nearly perfect.

When she saw Toby in the doorway, she stood at ease and greeted him. "It's about time you got out of bed."

Toby rubbed his eyes and yawned. "Why is everyone so energetic this morning?"

She pulled another arrow from the quiver, set up her shot, and drew the bow. She carefully aimed for the target then released the string with a snap. The arrow flew a hundred meters through the air and pierced through the center of the bullseye.

Witnessing this precision, Noraz chuckled. "Well done, Camryn. Your accuracy is improving." He glanced over at Toby, who stood weary-eyed and groggy. "Breakfast is over by the campfire. Once you've eaten, grab your armor and sword and meet me by the water well."

As soon as Toby ate and dressed, he carried his armor and sword out to the courtyard and dropped them at Noraz's feet.

Noraz glared at Toby with fiery eyes. "That armor belonged to my son, who appreciated the protection such wares offered him. Yet you throw it around, showing no respect or gratitude for the gift bestowed upon you." He huffed and shook his head. "Where does this disrespectful attitude of yours come from? You are full of anger, hate, and discontent, all of which make you dangerous if you don't learn to control your emotions. Pick up your sword."

Toby folded his arms, refusing to comply.

Noraz picked the sword up and shoved the pommel into Toby's chest. "The only way to learn how to use this weapon is to practice."

Toby rubbed his chest, now sore from the impact of the sword. He didn't appreciate being told what to do, but knew he had no choice if he and Camryn had any chance of getting out of here alive. With a heavy sigh, Toby held the sword in his hand and dragged it behind him as he followed Noraz to the center of the courtyard.

They situated themselves near a wooden practice dummy, where the Minotaur drew his own weapon. "When handling a sword, always have your feet at shoulder width." He demonstrated what a proper stance looked like. "And when you move, grip your sword firmly so you can handle it with ease."

Toby gripped the weapon with both hands and stood with his feet apart. He took a few practice swings, flailing the sword around wildly.

"Proper foot placement is key," Noraz instructed. "If not executed properly, your opponent will easily knock you over." He gently pushed on Toby's shoulder, who fell backwards and dropped his sword beside him.

Toby scowled at him. "Hey! Why'd you do that?"

Noraz couldn't help but laugh. "Balance is important. The moment you are on your back, you're as good as dead."

Toby stood upright and dusted himself off. "Teach me."

Noraz raised an eyebrow. "Oh? Now you want to learn?"

"Yes," Toby said, regaining possession of the sword. "Please. Show me how."

The Minotaur nodded in approval. "Very well. We'll begin with control." Noraz showed him correct foot placement. "You must be able to control your weapon. The more your foot touches the ground, the more balance you have, which gives you greater strength in your attacks. To maintain balance, try sliding your feet rather than lifting them."

Toby slid from side to side, keeping his feet as flat on the surface as he could. He was more able to control his sword this way.

"Keep your posture straight and your chest and torso forward. This will keep you from losing your balance during your swings and allow you to evade an attack."

Toby practiced his stance and got a feel for the weapon in his hand while Noraz corrected missteps and helped him refine his grip. Once Toby had good control and was able to move around freely, Noraz said, "Good. Now let's move on to execution."

To avoid injury and possible impalement, they started off using wooden swords with distinctive edges. This helped Toby build speed, perfect his physical techniques, and learn important concepts.

"Handling a sword is all about technique," Noraz said. "Which includes timing, distance, leverage, speed, and stamina. We'll start with some basic moves. Swing at me."

Toby lifted his sword and swung.

Noraz deflected his swing by holding the flat side of his sword in front of him. "This is a basic deflective action called a parry. When you parry, keep the blade close to you and use the flat part of your sword. Doing this properly can save your life. Doing it wrong can and will kill you." He demonstrated the move then had Toby try it. He caught on fairly quickly.

They sparred for a while with Noraz throwing swings and Toby deflecting them. After several hours, Toby leaned on his knees, panting.

Noraz patted him on the back. "You are doing well. Let's take a break and rest."

They set their swords in the nearby weapon rack and headed toward the water well.

As Toby lifted the bucket from the bottom of the well, his ring began to glow bright blue. "Hmm, that's odd," he said, loud enough for Noraz to hear him.

"What is?"

Toby held out his hand. "My ring. It's glowing blue."

Noraz gazed down into the well and saw a blue light illuminating from the water below. "The water is blue too."

Toby peered over the edge to look. Three wavy, horizontal lines appeared on one of the rocks at the edge of the well, along with some words written in a language Toby didn't understand. "Hey, Camryn," he hollered across the courtyard. "Come here for a minute."

Camryn set her bow down and joined them.

Toby pointed out the words to her. "Can you read this?"

She examined the engraving carefully—*Ecce lapis aqua.* "It means behold, the Water stone."

"Water stone?" Toby's eyes widened. "Do you suppose another one of the sacred stones is down there?"

Noraz huffed. "Perhaps. This land is well-hidden and has been unoccupied for decades. It would make sense for one of the stones to be concealed here."

Toby gazed down at the water, which emitted a bright blue light. "I have to get down there to get it." The rope coiled around the overhead pulley system gave him an idea. Toby reached for the rope and handed it to Noraz. "This will work."

"What are you doing with that?" Noraz asked, wondering what reckless act Toby was about to embark in.

"You're going to lower me down."

Noraz openly laughed, which echoed off the well walls. "I will do no such thing. For one thing, you will not fit in that bucket. And if that rope slips, not only will you fall into the well and possibly drown, you will also contaminate the only drinkable water within a hundred miles of here."

"But if one of the sacred stones is down there, I'm going to need it. Lower me down."

Camryn tried to talk some sense into him. "Toby, that's dangerous."

"And fighting some Firebeast isn't?" He looked Noraz straight in the eye. "You said yourself that these sacred stones are powerful."

"Yes, they are," Noraz replied.

"Then lower me down. I'm going to get that stone." Instead of using the water bucket as a descending device, Toby cut the bucket from the rope and created a harness. He tied it around himself securely and attached it to his belt.

Once the rope was secure, Noraz gripped the other end and eased Toby into the well.

The closer Toby got to the water, the brighter the light became. "I'm almost there. Just a little further," he called to Noraz.

Right as he said that, the rope, which had been worn and weakened from centuries of weathering, could no longer hold Toby's weight. It frayed and snapped. Toby plummeted a hundred feet to the bottom of the well and landed with a splash.

Camryn rushed to the edge and peeked down. "Toby?" she called to him. "Are you ok?"

Toby rose to the surface and spit water from his mouth. "I'm fine," his voice echoed off the walls. "The water absorbed my fall."

The ring on his finger became brighter. So did the light from the bottom of the well. Toby reached into the shallow water and gripped a glowing blue stone in his hand. "I have the stone," he said. "Now get me out of here."

"That might be a problem," Camryn noted, realizing that the only rope they had was now at the bottom of the well with Toby.

"Why?"

"The rope broke." She held up a five-foot section of rope, nowhere near long enough to reach the bottom of a 350-foot well. "This is all that's left."

"Hold on," Noraz said, coming up with a plan. He retrieved a coil of rope from a nearby hut and tied a bowline knot at the end of it. He then attached the opposite end to the cast iron pulley system and tossed the rope down to Toby. "Loop this through your belt and place both feet inside the knot. Grip the rope tightly, and I'll pull you up. Let me know when you're ready."

When Toby gave the signal, together, Noraz and Camryn pulled on the rope and slowly lifted Toby out of the well. When he reached the surface, they helped him to the edge and untied the ropes around him. Toby opened his palm. A bright blue stone, the size of a marble, glistened in his hand. "Now we have two stones. Two more to go." He handed the stone to Camryn, who in turn placed it in the leather pouch along with the green one.

Over the next several days, Noraz taught Toby offensive moves, focusing specifically on single-hand and two-handed cuts, strikes, thrusts, and lunges. He demonstrated each move and gave detailed explanations. "The force of a strike is determined by the velocity of the weapon on impact. Striking from the wrist is not nearly as powerful as striking from the shoulder, and striking with one arm is not as strong as striking with two." Noraz handed Toby a wooden sparring sword. "You ready?"

"Ready." Toby gripped the sword and swung aimlessly, trying to power the weapon with all of his strength. This quickly wore him out.

"You must have controlled intent," Noraz told him. "Be quick, but don't charge in recklessly. Keep your cool. If you are nervous or frightened, your opponent will take advantage of your lack of confidence and goad you into making a fatal mistake. Coordination, aim, focus, and follow-through are more important than brute physical force. Be sure of your attack and deliberate in your actions. You must act with speed and mental clarity and maintain control at all times. Use your whole body to place maximum impact on the target." He demonstrated with the practice dummy then had Toby give it another try.

It wasn't long before he got the hang of it.

For four full weeks, Noraz taught Toby full-contact strikes at a fixed target and controlled strikes at a mobile target. They worked on grappling and counter-attack combinations. As Toby gained more confidence, Noraz had him practice these techniques holding the sword in the opposite hand.

Once Toby gained more control and had a good handle on basic techniques, they switched to longblades. Toby started by using the practice dummy as a target before Noraz put on his armor and sparred with him.

Between sessions, Toby increased his stamina with aerobic exercises and gained strength through weight training. He ran through wilderness trails with full packs strapped on his back, lugged heavy logs around, and moved gear from one location to another. Over time, he became faster and stronger. Yet he had a hard time controlling his emotions. Anger made him impulsive, and fear led to indecisiveness.

In the middle of a practice session, Toby leaned on his knees to catch his breath. Before he even had time to think, Noraz whipped his body around and knocked him flat on his back.

"That's not fair. I wasn't ready," he argued.

"And do you think your opponent will wait for you to be ready?" Noraz warned. "Your lack of action will get you killed."

"I was just resting for a minute."

"You don't have time to rest. You must be on your guard at all times. Do not hesitate. Be aggressive, audacious, and take initiative. If you don't, it is highly likely that your opponent will take advantage and end the fight himself."

Toby nodded knowingly.

"Get up. Try again." Noraz held out his hand and lifted Toby off the ground.

On the thirtieth day, before the sun set, Noraz, Toby, and Camryn ventured into the wilderness carrying a hatchet, two daggers, and a bow and arrow. Noraz showed Toby how to forage for edible plants and berries and taught Camryn how to stay stealthy and use a bow and arrow for hunting. With his guidance, she was able to target a jackrabbit.

When they returned to camp, Noraz cleaned the rabbit and pierced it with a stick. He held the skewer over an open flame and barbecued the meat. The smell of smoke filled the camp.

While the meat cooked, Camryn separated figs and berries and refilled all of their water flasks then poured water into a bowl for the pup.

"Tomorrow we travel west," Noraz said.

Toby looked up. "We're leaving?"

"Yes. You must seek guidance from Erramus." He removed the rabbit from the flame, peeled off the skin, and portioned out the meat between the three of them.

Right as Toby was about to take a bite, Noraz drew his sword and pointed it directly at his chest. Startled, Toby stumbled backwards and fell in the dirt. With his hand over his pounding heart, he said, "What is wrong with you? You almost gave me a heart attack."

"I told you to always be on your guard," Noraz warned him. "Never let down your defenses."

Camryn giggled at Toby's ghost white face. "Are your pants still dry?"

"Shut up," he snapped.

With a chuckle, Noraz sheathed his sword and carefully placed it in the weapon rack. "You have learned much, young Guardian. You are ready."

"What about defense?" Toby asked, not feeling prepared. "How do I defend myself against this Firebeast? No doubt he's bigger and stronger than me, and lord knows what kind of attacks he'll throw my direction."

"Your best defense is evasion." Noraz grabbed his plate and tore off a chunk of rabbit meat. "Watch his movements and learn when and how he strikes. Displace his attacks with perfectly timed counter strikes at vulnerable spots. Thrust, cut, grapple, throw rocks, kick sand in his eyes, whatever is effective. Use the physical environment to your advantage. Gain higher ground if you can. Force him to have the sun in his eyes, which will make it much harder for him to see you. Do whatever you can to protect yourself. Natural barriers such as cliffs or walls cut off mobility and escape routes. Trap him in enclosed spaces. Create a distraction, seek cover, then close in. Moving targets are harder to strike, so be in constant motion. Trust your gut feeling and be aware at all times. Following these steps could potentially save your life and allow you to deliver the winning blow. Remember, you are fighting for your life. Do not hold back."

"I understand."

Noraz gave a confident nod. "I have nothing left to teach you. Only Erramus has the knowledge to guide you further. She lives in the temple of Moria. At day break, we travel west. Gather your supplies and prepare for your journey."

"You're coming with us, aren't you?"

"I will take you only as far as the temple, then I must return to the labyrinth. Erramus will guide you from there."

Chapter 7

They ventured out of the barren desert land into a jungle full of broad-leafed trees. An ancient city, cloaked in dappled tree shadows, was locked in the muscular embrace of a vast root system. Vines grew up the crumbling walls, and a few trees rooted themselves into the decrepit stone buildings, towers, and tombs. The whole city had been swallowed by the jungle.

"These are the ruins of Moria," the Minotaur said. "Former home of the Aradatha tribe. Erramus is the only one who remains here. Her whereabouts are unknown to most, as she stays hidden."

Crumbled rock sculptures lay in pieces on the ground, and the edge of the walls were covered in black soot, the same soot that Toby and Camryn saw when they first crossed the waterfall barrier. "Did the Firebeast do this?" Toby asked, rubbing his hand across the wall, getting soot all over his fingers.

"Yes. As soon as the Treelings fled, the Firebeast gained control over the Fire element and went around Gelnoff setting fire to every village."

"I thought you said he didn't know how to control the elements?"

"He doesn't, with the exception of Fire. He uses it to satisfy his rage. This is why it's important that we stop him. His anger grows stronger and he becomes more and more unpredictable every day, which increases Fire's destructive powers. Without the other elements to counteract that power, it's only a matter of time before Gelnoff is burned to oblivion, along with all of its inhabitants."

Although Toby knew very little about the clans and tribes who lived in this land, he actually felt sympathy for their plight.

"He kidnapped my children by trapping them within a wall of fire. The wall was impassible, and I could not come to their aid. They tried to fight him off, but he was too powerful, and they could not overtake him. All I could do was helplessly watch as he carried them away to his lair." Noraz hung his head. As strong and tough as he was, Toby swore he saw a tear roll down his cheek. "I was not strong enough to stop him. Too many times he has taken tribes of children to his fiery prison. Several have tried to free themselves from his torture, but those who have tried, end up dead. It will take someone with extreme mental strength to overcome him and get the children back. Someone who knows how to channel the elements. Someone who can take Fire's power away from him and use it the way it was intended. You can defeat him, and I believe you will. But I cannot go with you. I have done my part to get you this far. You must continue the journey on your own."

"You can't just leave us here."

"Seek Erramus. She will give you further instructions."

Although Toby originally felt intimidated by Noraz, he now felt a connection with him and didn't want him to leave. "Noraz..."

"You must continue without me," Noraz interjected, not allowing Toby to finish his sentence. "Continue due west and you will find the temple. Remember everything I've taught you, and listen to Erramus. She is wise. Go now, and godspeed, young Guardian." Noraz turned and walked away, leaving Toby, Camryn, and the wolf to venture on their own.

"Now what?" Toby asked, feeling abandoned and unwanted. "I thought he wanted to help us?"

"You heard what he said. He did his part. Now he's passing the torch to whoever this Erramus person is."

"How are we supposed to find her?"

"We go west, just like Noraz said."

Deep within the ruins, a huge stone structure lie hidden, surrounded by a moat of stagnant, algae-infested water. Its towers and closed courtyards were clogged with tree roots, and the blackened walls were carpeted with lichen, moss, and creeping plants. Shrubs sprouted from the roof, and hundred-year-old trees towered overhead, filtering the sunlight and casting a greenish cloud over the whole scene. It was an eerie, yet majestic sight.

Just outside the structure, several crescents, circles, trefoils, and interwoven branches were carved on the front of a wall. Camryn stopped and stared at them. "This is the temple."

"How do you know?"

She pointed to the inscriptions on the wall. "Look."

Sure enough, the same symbols they'd seen many times throughout this journey were carved into this wall. Toby's ring began to glow again, and a spiral symbol appeared on the surface. "I think you're right, but how do we get inside?"

"See if there's a keyhole or a passageway somewhere."

They searched the surrounding area, lifting stones, digging through rubble, and checking around plants for any signs of an entrance. Hidden behind a thick patch of foliage, Toby discovered a decrepit, moss covered doorway which had cracked and crumbled under the pressure of growing roots and decades of weathering. The doorway was surrounded by an intricately detailed arch with ten-foot pillars on each side. Above the arch was a sculpted image of a tree with interconnected branches. Being careful not to lose his footing, Toby stepped closer to get a better look at it. On one of the pillars, he found a triple spiral carved into the stone. "Camryn!" he yelled, hoping to get her attention. "Come over here. I think I found something."

Camryn quickly joined him.

"Look. It's the same symbol that's on my ring." He held up his hand to show her. "This has to be the entrance."

"Probably."

"How do we open it?"

Camryn flipped through the tome for more information, but couldn't find anything. She dug further by snooping around the archway for other symbols or clues. The words *solum introitus* were written across the archway. "Entrance by invitation only," she read.

"An invitation from who?" Toby stared at the ring on his finger, which now glowed bright yellow. "Do you think this ring is our ticket in?"

"It did get us through the waterfall. It's certainly worth a try."

He pointed his ring toward the archway, but nothing happened. "Hmm, wonder what I'm doing wrong?"

"Maybe there's a code or a chant or some kind of secret password that unlocks the door."

The Guardian

Right as Camryn said that, the ground began to rumble and shake beneath them, causing loose stones to fall from the temple and crash to the jungle floor. Dodging falling debris, Toby dove to his right. With a loud roar, the ground split open, sucking Camryn into a hole, feet first. Her scream was the last thing Toby heard.

"Camryn!" Toby tried to run after her, but with all the boulders and rocks tumbling to the ground and shattering, it was difficult for him to stay on his feet.

The ground trembled and cracked for several minutes before it finally stopped quaking.

The wolf charged toward a pile of crumbled stones and barked.

Rising to his feet, Toby followed him. He dug his way through the debris to a giant hole in the ground. Looking down, a deep spiral staircase twisted endlessly into a dark, underground abyss. "Camryn, are you down there?"

"Yes," her voice echoed in response. "And I'm alright."

Toby breathed a sigh of relief. "Where are you?"

"I'm not sure, but I think I found the entrance to the temple. Get down here."

Cautiously, Toby placed his foot on the first step. Once he was certain the staircase was stable, he climbed all the way down, making endless turns as he descended into the pit. Candlelight flickered and made shadowy figures on the walls of the deep corridor.

When Toby's feet hit the floor, the flickering lights from the candles cast a silhouette of Camryn's shadow on the wall. "That was the weirdest thing I've ever seen. How did…" He stopped dead in his tracks when he realized the enormous size of the room they were in. "Whoa. What is this place?"

Although many of the temple's narrow corridors were blocked off by jumbled piles of carved stone blocks dislodged by large root systems, this room was completely intact. Life-sized statues stood tall around them, and rock formations with Gaelic symbols occupied every corner of the room. It looked like some kind of shrine.

"Now this is cool," Toby said, awed by the symbols carved into the walls and the lifelike facial features on the statues.

Corridors and passageways went off in every direction. "How do we know which way to go?" Toby asked, trying to make heads or tails of this interconnected cave system.

On the opposite side of the room, Camryn spotted a spiral pattern just like the one etched on Toby's sword. She pivoted her body that direction. "I think we should go this way."

Toby's ring and sword glowed in bright green, confirming Camryn's choice. "I think you're right."

They descended down a steep stone staircase to a room full of carved statues. A corridor on the other side was illuminated by torches. Although they had no idea where it led, they followed the long, curvy passageway into an adjoining cavern. This room was bigger than the previous one, and smack in the center was a rock formation similar to the one they saw by the river. The only difference was each of these stones had a crystal glowing inside it. One was green, one was blue, one was yellow, and the other was red.

From behind a pillar, a female figure dressed in a green cloak entered the room. She had ram's horns on her head, pointed ears like an elf, and wore a large pendant with five interlocking circles around her neck. A golden elvish crown decorated her green-tinted hair. As soon as Toby and

Camryn entered the chamber, she pointed a staff at them. A gust of wind pushed them backwards.

"Who are you, and how did you get into my temple?" she asked.

Toby replied, "Noraz sent us."

"The Minotaur?"

"Yes. We're looking for Erramus."

"What do you want with her?"

"Noraz said she would help us. He said Erramus could show me how to channel the elements. Do you know who she is? Can you tell us where to find her?"

The female figure pointed her staff at several freestanding torches, each of which ignited on its own. "What makes you think the sage has the time or the desire to help the likes of you?"

Any woman who had the power to set torches aflame simply by pointing a stick at them must have been powerful. Toby had to tread carefully. "Please, Ma'am."

"Tell me why I should help you."

Based on that remark, and the fact that she could control air and fire with minimal effort, Toby asked, "You're Erramus?"

"I am." She set her staff against the wall. "What do you know about the elements?"

"We saw the elemental stones near the river, spoke to some druid named Tyree, and found this sword in the water." Toby pulled his sword from the sheath and showed it to the sage.

"The sword of Aonghus is the most powerful weapon ever made," she said.

Toby raised his eyebrows. "Seriously?"

"Yes. The strength of each element is stored within its blades. But you cannot channel that strength without the elemental crystals."

"Maybe these will help." Toby pulled out a leather pouch and dumped two shiny marbled-sized stones into his hand—one blue, one green.

"Where did you get those?"

"I found the blue one at the bottom of a well, and Noraz gave me the other one. He said you'd know what to do with them."

She cupped the stones in her hand. "These gems have been lost for centuries. Noraz was wise to send you here. May I see the sword?"

He placed the handle in her hand, and she carefully examined the blade. "This is beautiful. You say you found this in the water?"

"Yes."

"Where?"

"In the river, right on the border of Alderwood."

Her entire face lit up. "That's where they hid it. Clever creatures." She held the green stone between her thumb and forefinger and carefully slid it into a small indention on the front of the crossguard. It stuck to the metal like a magnet. She turned the sword over and did the same with the blue stone. The sword's blade immediately illuminated.

Toby's eyes gazed at the bright light. He had no idea the sword he had learned how to use could do that. "Whoa."

"The full power of the sword cannot be channeled without all four stones. The red and yellow stones are missing. You must find them before the Firebeast does."

"Where are they?"

"I do not know. The stones were separated and hidden centuries ago, to keep the Firebeast from acquiring them.

Only the Treelings know of their whereabouts, but no one knows where the Treelings are."

"Then how are we supposed to find them?"

"The elements will guide you, if you channel their energy."

"Can you show me how?"

"I can," the sage said. "But only if you are open to learn."

Toby bobbed his head. "I'm open. Please teach me."

She set the sword down and the light disappeared.

"Why did it stop glowing?"

"The sword's power can only be released if in the hands of one who has the capability to channel the elements. Let me show you how to do it." She led him to the middle of the rock structure and positioned his body in such a way that his arms were straight out to his sides. "Keep your back straight and hold your arms out to your sides. The flow of energy from every element connects everything that exists, and you, a living being, are taking in this energy at every moment. In order to channel that energy, you must first learn to recognize it."

"How do I do that?"

"Through visualization. Let your unconscious mind merge with the universe. Become one with nature. Let's start with Earth. Hone in on the light filtering through the trees. Listen to the birds, smell the flowers, see the green grass. Close your eyes and focus your thoughts toward the energy center of the element."

Toby closed his eyes and tried to visualize this in his mind, but had a hard time staying focused.

"You must have sustained thought. Be mindful of the natural energy around you. Calling in the energy from the element will start the energy flowing through you. When you summon the energy, you will see it coming into your body—up from the earth, down from above you, and from the atmosphere all around you. Bring the greatest measure of energy into your own energy field. As you do, you will see the energy flow into you and move through your body towards your shoulders, down your arms, and into your hands."

Wisps of green light flowed all around Toby. Chills developed, and his hands felt warm and tingly. "I feel cold," he said. "And my hands are numb."

"Do not speak," the sage instructed. "Switch off every distraction and stay focused. Visualize nature without distortion."

He cleared his mind and tried to imagine trees and grass and a field of flowers. Energy flowed through him, making him calm and more conscientious of his surroundings. His ring turned a bright shade of green.

"Take in the full sensation of the element. Feel the energy coming into you from all around. Let it flow through your body like water filling a glove. You should feel a tingling, or even a sensation of heat, as the energy flows and collects in your hands."

"I feel it," he said.

"Good. Now use that energy to gain mental clarity. Focus."

Toby could clearly visualize a mountain with a river running through it. This river was surrounded by dense trees. "I see a village in the mountains."

"Let the element guide you. Follow the image you see."

"I can't. I..." Without fully understanding what was happening, he dropped to his knees. Instantly, the ring returned to its original golden luster, and the energy left his body, leaving him winded and covered in sweat.

"Breathe. Let the energy leave your body slowly."

Toby took a few big breaths, clearing his lungs and releasing the energy within him.

"Well done. You channeled your first element."

"I saw places I've never seen before, like in a dream."

The sage clarified, "The elements are speaking to you."

"Speaking to me? But I didn't hear anything."

"The elements don't speak in a sense you are accustomed to. They guide you through images. You need to learn to control your thoughts to maintain those images."

Toby combed his fingers through his hair and desperately fought to catch his breath.

"Rest for a moment then let's move on to Water."

Through visualization, Toby was able to channel each element one by one. First Water, then Wind, and finally Fire. He had more control of Earth and Water than he did over the other two elements, but he was learning different visualization techniques to better help him channel Wind's energy. Because the Fire element was unpredictable and unstable, it was the hardest for him to control. Channeling Fire increased his irritability and made him want to destroy things. This feeling only lasted for a minute or two before the entire element lost its strength and burned out.

"Fire requires the most concentration," the sage told him. "And it will quickly burn out without fuel. Fire thrives on activity and is better channeled while in motion. Channeling the elements, when practiced correctly, can become the source from which all actions flow—eating, sleeping, breathing, and even thinking. Everything around you gets its energy from one or more of the elements. You must learn to not only control these elements, but combine them to gain the most energy from them. Knowing the strengths of each element helps you to better channel them."

"Now I get it," Camryn said as she pulled the tome from her bag. "This is a recipe book. It tells you how to combine the elements and pull from their strengths." She turned to the page that listed all the different element combinations.

Erramus bowed her head. "You are wise beyond your years, child. Study the tome. Learn what the elements can do."

Over the course of the next few days, Toby became less moody and more patient. He was able to channel individual elements and learned to better control his thoughts and actions. He gained more control of Fire and could easily channel Earth and Water, not only from the power of the crystals, but from nature itself. He practiced with each element until he perfected it then moved on to the next one. It wasn't long before he could pull the energy from each individual element.

"To draw out the full power of the sword, it must be in your hands at the same time all four elements are channeled, otherwise it has no more strength than any other weapon," Erramus said. "Very few have been able to successfully channel all four elements at once."

"Do you think I'll be able to do it?" Toby asked, feeling more confident about this task.

"It will take complete clarity of mind and a total state of focus to channel every element at once, but I believe you can do it. You must maintain this state of mind at all times and not let fear or doubt or anger distract you. Even the slightest distraction will cause imbalance and you will lose control."

The Guardian

Five days after entering the temple, the sage directed Toby and Camryn to go south, through the ruins and into the valley of Gist. They restocked their supplies and made their way back up the spiral staircase to the surface, where the wolf pup stood guard waiting for them. As soon as they exited the temple, the ground grumbled underneath them, and the ancient stone structure returned to its original state. The fallen boulders realigned with one another, the underground staircase sunk back into the ground, and the earth and plants reclaimed the area as if nothing happened.

"Every time I turn around weird things happen around here," Toby said. "Trees talk, the ground cracks under our feet for no apparent reason, and staircases appear out of nowhere. We keep running into strange creatures, finding unusual objects, and crumbled buildings miraculously glue themselves back together again. What kind of place is this?"

"A magical place, Toby. Truly magical."

Chapter 8

The ruins of Moria were full of ancient houses, archways, bridges, and towers. A dried up riverbed ran through the middle of the city, and vines covered almost every inch of the exterior wall. Moss-covered rocks formed natural barriers around buildings, and stone paths created roads in and out of the area. Tall broad-leafed trees provided shade, but with no water or moisture present, Toby couldn't figure out how these trees were able to grow.

"Maybe the plants around here don't need water," Camryn suggested.

"That doesn't make any sense. The druid of Alderwood told us that the trees draw in water from the soil, but it hasn't rained one day since we've been here. Each place we've visited is drastically different than the next. How can the landscape go from barren and dry to thriving with plant life within only a few miles? Nothing about this place makes sense."

As they hiked further down the path, a distant voice cried out, "Help me! Please, someone help me!"

"Who said that?" Camryn looked around for signs of life.

The voice hollered again, "Please get me out of here before the Hawkstrich returns and eats me!"

Toby, Camryn, and the wolf followed the frantic voice to the other side of the ruins. Inside a cage made of heavy logs and large boulders, a short, thick-skinned creature was huddled in a corner hugging his knees. At first, Toby thought it was a rock, until he saw a pair of eyes staring at him.

"Get me out of this cage. The Hawkstrich will be back any minute."

"What's a Hawkstrich?" Toby asked.

A high pitched screech from the sky above quickly answered that question. Casting shadows over them, a grey and white bird about the size of a griffin swooped down with his talons spread wide open. Toby and Camryn ducked just in time to dodge his attack.

"What is that thing?" Toby scanned the sky, searching for the giant bird.

"I told you he was coming back," the wrinkly rock creature cried. "Get me out of here or we'll all die!"

This giant bird had a round body, long, skinny legs, and a thin, extended neck. It was awkward and gangly like an ostrich, but unlike an ostrich, this bird could fly. Its long neck bobbed with every wing stroke, yet it was surprisingly graceful in the air. The disproportionate bird with its twenty foot wingspan, six-inch talons, and sharp, pointy beak swooped down again, but this time it gripped a log with its chubby toes and carried it up to the sky.

Toby looked to the left and the right, hoping to spot the winged creature. No signs of the bird anywhere. "Where did it go?"

The wolf pup yipped, and within seconds, the long-legged bird hovered overhead, staring Toby down with eerie, fiery eyes. It squawked once more then loosened its grip on the log. The heavy log barreled toward Toby, gaining speed with every second. Toby managed to dive out of the way right before the log smashed into the ground.

"That bird is trying to kill me," he said, and he pulled his sword from its sheath, gripping it with both hands.

The caged creature agreed. "If we don't leave now, he'll eat us both."

Toby wasn't about to let a funny-looking bird intimidate him. He took a fighting stance, ready to ward off the animal. The bird dove at him with outstretched talons. Toby used the flat end of his sword to deflect the bird's attack. "Camryn!" he called to his sister. "See if you can find a way to set the little guy free while I distract this bird!"

While Toby fought off the Hawkstrich, Camryn yanked and tugged at the rocks and logs, trying to loosen the enclosure. The structure was pieced together tightly, and no amount of tugging seemed to dislodge the rocks. "It won't budge," she said.

"Keep trying!"

With its talons bared and mouth wide open, the lanky bird spread its wings and flew straight for Toby. To avoid being scooped into the bird's mouth, Toby dodged to the right. The bird landed on the ground and smacked Toby in the head with its wing.

Toby stumbled a bit before he regained his footing. "Oh yeah? You wanna play rough?" He held the sword firmly in his hand. "Bring it on, bird brain."

The Hawkstrich screeched and pecked at Toby's feet. Toby evaded him by counterattacking with his sword. The bird tried again, but this time it made contact with Toby's shin.

Toby wailed in pain. With blood dripping down his leg, he eyeballed the bird straight on, circling around him in a challenging showdown. "That's it, bird. You're going down." He tried to ignore the pain in his leg as he thrust at the bird's chest. The Hawkstrich pecked at Toby's sword, leaving beak marks on the metal blade. This didn't deter Toby in any way. He struck again, making contact with the bird's right wing, injuring it. Unable to fly with any kind of stability, the bird squawked and stomped its feet, like a ravaged bull ready to charge.

Toby stood his ground.

With his eyes focused on Toby, the bird raced toward him, squealing. Toby did the only thing he could think of, he held the sword straight in front of him and allowed the Hawkstrich to be the cause of his own demise. The bird charged right into the blade.

With a gasping breath, the Hawkstrich's body went limp and collapsed to the ground. Toby retrieved his sword and wiped the blade clean with the dead bird's feathers. "There. One less creepy creature to worry about."

"Oh, thank you," the rock creature said. "Thank you."

Toby stared at the creature oddly. "Who or what are you?"

"I'm Grud, and I'm a rock troll. Now, please release me from this cage."

"Hold on a second. Why should we let you out? What do we get from it?"

"If you release me, I'll reward you."

"Reward us with what?"

"I have plenty of plunder that I will gladly share with you, but you have to set me free to see it."

Toby cocked his head. "Why should we believe you?"

Camryn cut in, "We can't just leave him here. He'll dehydrate and starve to death."

"Yes, yes," the troll added. "I can offer you food, shelter, and I will lead you to fresh drinking water."

Not trusting this creature, Toby pointed the tip of his blade at the troll's chest. "Alright, but if you're lying..."

The rock troll wore an innocent smirk. "Me? Lie? What would I gain by lying? You saved my life, perhaps I can return the favor."

After careful consideration, Toby decided to help Camryn break down the rocky structure. With a few tugs and pushes, they were able to knock a few logs loose. The grey-skinned troll immediately crawled out of his entrapment. "I owe you a great debt. Please, come with me, and I shall repay you."

The three-foot, floppy-eared rock troll had rugged features, like stone worn down by the weather. The creature was unkempt, so much so that moss had taken root on its skin. A single strand of hair poked out of its head. As they headed south down a rocky path, the troll waddled from side to side.

Camryn stared at the troll's backside and couldn't help but laugh.

Toby glared at her as if she'd lost her mind. "What is so funny?"

The troll's knob-kneed legs barely held up its round, moss-covered body. "Look at his weeble-wobble legs. They can't support his own body weight."

Now that Camryn mentioned it, the troll did look funny when he walked. Toby giggled right along with her.

The landscape around them began to drastically shift from tall trees and soft moss to charcoal stumps and charred stones. The air around them reeked of sulfur. "Ugh, that smells awful." Toby held his nose between his thumb and finger so he wouldn't have to endure the stench.

Fire seemed to dominate the land of Gelnoff. Almost every area they'd visited had evidence of fire damage— singed tree trunks, sooty rocks, and ash-covered surfaces. Toby leaned toward Camryn and said, "Have you noticed that everything around here has been burned to some extent?"

Camryn shrugged off this information. "So?"

"So, did it ever occur to you that maybe this Firebeast is a vicious fire-breathing dragon?"

"It's not a dragon, Toby."

"How can you be so sure? Based on the evidence and the way the people around here talk about this beast, it sure sounds like a dragon. Dragons are enormous and fierce and always hungry. They will eat anything, especially young, human flesh like me."

A few miles down the road, they crossed through a narrow path with high cliff walls on both sides. At first glance, it looked like the entire area was covered with snow. But upon further examination, delicate white crystals formed a thick, crusty layer across the surface of the soil. The ground was so dry, it cracked, and the salt-like crystals crunched under their feet. The blistering sun caused heat waves to ripple across the path. The dry, barren environment was far too harsh to allow any plants or people to survive.

"It is so hot here." Toby's sweat evaporated in the heat, and the high temperature made the wolf pup pant. "How can anyone live in this horrid environment? This is the most miserable place I've ever seen. I'm going to shrivel up and die if I don't get water soon."

"Not much further now," the troll told them. "Just a few more yards to the river."

"What river? There's nothing around here but salt and clay."

They trekked up a steep hill that overlooked a valley. The air became thick around them and a swirling cloud hovered overhead. Mist rose from the surface of the ground, which made it much more difficult to see where they were going. Through the mist, Toby looked out over the horizon. Thick fog blanketed the valley. "It's eerie and creepy here. What is this place?"

"My home is not far from here. Just a few more feet 'til we reach the river," the troll said.

They descended down the hill. A stream flowed between their feet, and large raindrops pelted them from all angles, which made the path dangerously slippery. Water seeped up from the ground and their shoes squished into the soft, thick mud. The wet environment formed water droplets on their skin and soaked them from their hair all the way to their feet.

The area around them carried the pungent smell of rotting vegetation, wet soil, and mold, and the water-logged soil made a slurping sound when Camryn pulled her foot from the mud. She curled her lip in disgust. "This place is repulsive."

With her next step, Camryn's feet slipped from under her, and she fell backwards into the mud. The steepness and slipperiness of the incline made her slide all the way down to the bottom of the hill, where she abruptly landed in a puddle and came to a stop. She was covered in mud and soaked from head to toe.

Toby rolled with laughter.

Camryn didn't find this nearly as amusing as Toby seemed to think it was. She combed her hair out of her eyes with her fingers and tried to wipe mud off her face, which only smeared it more. "This isn't funny."

Before Toby had a chance to respond, the ground gave way underneath him and swept him and the wolf pup down the hill. He landed face first in the puddle, right next to Camryn. Toby lifted his head and water dripped down his face and chin.

Camryn snorted with amusement. "How's mud taste?"

He spit muddy water from his mouth and rose to his knees. "Yuk."

The wolf pup shook water off himself while Toby wiped mud from his eyes.

A steadily flowing river blocked the path ten feet in front of them. They rose to their feet and did their best to clean themselves up. With rapids raging through the entire width of the river, there was no way they could cross it.

The rock troll, who somehow managed to avoid the mud slide, came up behind them and said, "We must travel down river. Follow me. I'll lead you."

They followed the riverbank to the west until they came to an old, rickety bridge that connected one side of the river to the other. Toby thought the troll was going to take them over the wooden structure, but instead of crossing the river, they crawled underneath the bridge into a hidden doorway.

While the wolf stood watch, the troll lit a nearby torch, which quickly illuminated a hollow crawlspace. "Come inside. You'll be warm here."

They crawled through the opening to an underground room with a grass and clay covered ceiling. The room was just tall enough to allow Camryn and Toby to move around comfortably without hitting their heads. The modest accommodations allowed little personal space, and the dirt-covered floor wasn't particularly cozy, but at least it offered a place of solace to keep them dry for the night. In the center of the room, a small dining table, set with wooden bowls and cups, invited them to sit down for a meal. Since they hadn't eaten much today, Toby's stomach grumbled.

A black wood-burning stove filled the far corner of the room. The troll opened the stove door, threw some paper and kindling inside, and lit a fire. Warmth quickly filled the room. The troll grabbed two towels from a nearby shelf and handed them to Camryn and Toby. "Clean up and dry your clothes. I'll prepare us something to eat." He carried a black cauldron, almost as big as he was, over to the stove. He filled it with water and left it there to boil.

When the troll disappeared to another room, Camryn and Toby peeled off layers of mud-soaked clothes. Toby took off the belt that held his sword and leaned it against the wall. Then he set his muddy shoes on the floor in front of the stove and allowed the heat to dry them. His shirt came off next, which he hung on a drying rack on the opposite side of the room.

Camryn removed her pack and set it on the floor. She unfastened the latch and opened the pouch to make sure the contents had not been damaged in the mudslide. Although the leather cover on the tome was wet, the pages were still intact. She wiped the cover off with a towel and set it aside. She dumped out the rest of the contents, including the key they retrieved from the purple stone, and put them in a pile by the tome.

"Are you sure we can trust this guy?" Toby said.

Camryn set the bag on the floor in front of the fire to let it dry. "I don't see why we shouldn't."

The troll returned with two furry blankets. He handed one to Camryn and one to Toby. "This part of Gelnoff can be dangerous. You must watch your step."

"Yeah." Toby said, annoyed that the troll hadn't warned them earlier. "Now you tell us."

"What were you doing in Moria? That area has been abandoned for years."

Not fully trusting this rock troll, Toby said, "We were visiting an old friend who lives near there."

The troll stared intently at the pile of objects Camryn had laid out on the floor, focused particularly on the shiny key. "I see. Although I don't recall anyone living in those parts." Then his eyes wandered to Toby's sword, fascinated by the crystals embedded on the handle.

Camryn covered the sword with a towel then removed her wet clothes and hung them on the dying rack. "We were just passing through on our way to the valley."

"Why are you traveling to the valley? What is there that you seek?

Without thinking, Camryn blurted out, "We're looking for the Firebeast."

The troll filled a bowl with drinking water and gave it to the wolf pup. "Most strive to make themselves invisible to him, yet you actively seek his presence. Why?"

Toby sneered at Camryn, wishing she would keep her big mouth shut. "We have some business with him."

The rock troll snorted under his breath. "Business with the Firebeast will lead to either imprisonment or death."

Toby wrapped himself up in the blanket to stay warm. "Why are you so interested?"

"The treasures I have, the Firebeast will gladly take. Which reminds me." He reached under a burlap cloth and pulled out a bow and quiver. "I offer you this bow for saving me from the Hawkstrich."

Camryn gladly took it. "Thank you."

"I obtained it during the Element Wars."

"The Element Wars?" Toby asked, scooting a bit closer to the stove to soak in more heat.

"Do you not know of the conflict between the Treelings and the Firebeast? Our land is in this current state of disarray because of the outcome of that battle. In the peak of the fight, the Treelings fled and disappeared. To this day, their whereabouts are unknown. Until the Firebeast finds them, he will continue to torment every village in Gelnoff. But there are almost no tribes left. He has either kidnapped or killed them all, and those who are still alive have fled or gone into hiding to evade his wrath."

"Why are you still here?" Toby asked curiously.

"I give him no reason to target me." The troll placed a biscuit on each plate then pulled a jug out of the cupboard. He popped the cork and poured blue liquid into each cup. "The valley you seek is upriver from here. Follow the riverbank to the east and you will find it. But now, eat. Rest. By sunrise, the storm should let up and you can be on your way."

Before turning in for the night, Camryn repacked her bag and set it against the wall by Toby's sword. She leaned her newly acquired bow and quiver beside them. "We must be getting close," she told Toby.

Toby found a straw-stuffed pillow and rested his head on it. "I don't know if I trust this troll, Camryn. Trolls don't have the reputation of being friendly or helpful. They pillage valuables, and some have been known to rip trees from their roots and hurl boulders hundreds of feet in the air. I even read stories where trolls eat people. I wouldn't be surprised if he's the one who conjured up this storm to trap us here."

"Why would he do that? We saved his life. Surely he wouldn't try to harm us."

As smart at Camryn was, Toby was sometimes surprised by her lack of common sense. "You don't really believe that, do you? You are far too trusting. I'm going to have one eye open all night, looking right at him."

Chapter 9

In the morning, after a breakfast of porridge and honeysuckle tea, Camryn and Toby gathered their belongings and traveled upriver with the wolf pup. Several hours into their journey, the air became much colder. Toby rubbed his hands over his arms to warm himself. "It is freezing out here. Are you sure this is the right way?"

"It must be. The troll said to go upriver. We've been following the river the whole time."

The path they were following became steeper and rockier with every step. The air was thinner, chilling wind wisped all around them, and snowflakes fell from the sky. A layer of thick ice formed on the surface of the river. As they hiked further up the mountain, Toby began to question Camryn's navigational skills. "I don't think we're going the right way. There isn't a valley anywhere near here."

"The valley is probably on the other side of the mountain."

One thing was for certain, they had experienced almost every type of weather condition imaginable in this strange land. One minute Toby was sweating to death and dying from dehydration, the next he was suffering from frostbite.

Around the next bend, a high-pitched scream echoed off the ravine walls.

"What is that?" Toby asked.

"It sounds like a bird." Camryn led them further up the path where the screech became louder.

Around the corner, they encountered a large-winged bird. It squawked and flapped its wings, trying to break free from whatever its foot was caught on.

"It looks like it's stuck. Let's go help it," Camryn suggested.

"Why must you insist on coming to the aid of every animal we run into?"

"Because it's stuck. You don't want it to suffer and die, do you?"

Toby rolled his eyes and followed her.

Although the wolf pup hunched down and growled, Camryn approached the animal. This giant bird had blue and green feathers, a bright yellow beak, and thick, orange legs. One of its feet was stuck in a layer of ice.

As Camryn got closer to the creature, the bird whipped its head around and stared at her with its big, golden eyes. In a state of panic, the animal yanked at its foot and tried to peck at the ice with its beak.

"It's alright," she reassured the frightened animal. "I'm not going to hurt you."

At first the animal was cautious. It jerked its head from side to side and squawked at her. But as Camryn reached her hand out to touch the bird's wing, the giant eagle allowed her to touch it. "If you can help me get my foot loose, I will be eternally grateful."

Camryn took a step back. She wasn't expecting this giant bird to speak to her. "You can talk," she said.

The Guardian

"Of course I can talk. I am Aakesh." The eagle lowered its head and bowed. "Leader of the Aquila clan. Don't suppose you have a way to loosen this ice, do you?"

"She doesn't," Toby said as he drew his sword. "But I might." He walked to the river's edge and placed the tip of his sword on the ice. Wisps of red light swirled all around him. Energy traveled through his body all the way to the blade of the sword, which made the sword illuminate in bright crimson. The glowing light produced enough heat to melt the ice and allow the eagle to pull his foot free.

"Thank you," the eagle said, shaking water from its foot. "I owe you my life."

"How did you get yourself stuck?" Camryn asked.

"I landed by the river to catch a fish and my foot got lodged between two rocks. The river froze around it, leaving me trapped in the ice. If you two wouldn't have come along, who knows how long I would have been stuck there." He stretched his wings and took a few hops. "What are you doing on this mountain?"

"We're trying to get to the valley."

The eagle gave them a curious stare. "You are a day's journey from the valley, and in this weather, with the sun setting soon, you will freeze to death out here."

Toby sneered at Camryn. "I told you we were going the wrong way." He rubbed his arms to ward off the cold.

"I know of a hidden sanctuary near here where you can seek shelter for the night. Come with me. I'll guide you."

They followed a mountain path through a barren area of snow. It was covered with sturdy shrubs, wildflowers, and lichen. At the top of a cliff, the eagle directed them to a narrow opening that led to a hidden entryway at the base of a rock structure.

"I can travel no further," the eagle said. "But should you need my services, simply say my name, and I will fly to your aid."

"Where are you going?" Camryn asked.

"I must patrol the skies of Gelnoff. Wicked forces are among us, and it is my job to keep the remaining clans safe. Good luck to you." He bowed, outstretched his wings, and flew off into the horizon.

Toby, Camryn, and the wolf descended down a path to a round archway. The scent of campfire smoke and the distant bleating of sheep lingered in the air. They proceeded down a tiered stone staircase to a secluded mountain village. All kinds of creatures—Minotaurs, human figures with ram's horns, small wrinkled men with pointy ears, yellow pixies with crystal wings, goat-headed men with antlers, elves with leafy fronds protruding from their heads, and large blue and green eagles—filled the streets. Some carried water from wells to cottages while others chopped wood, baked bread, and looked after young ones. White feathered peacocks, small furry rodents with thick tails, wooly sheep, brown tailed rabbits, and a variety of unusual birds frolicked around the courtyard. Children tended to the animals, and every creature lived and worked together harmoniously. An eagle, a goat man, an elf, and an old bearded man wearing a white cloak gathered around a fire in the center of the village. They passed around a tobacco pipe as they conversed.

Toby and Camryn entered the village and all heads turned. The bearded man rose to his feet, holding out his staff to block their path. "Do not take another step."

Camryn and Toby stopped dead in their tracks.

"Who are you and why have you come here?"

Camryn took it upon herself to address these men. "I'm Camryn, and this is my brother, Toby. Aakesh sent us this way. He told us we could find shelter here."

"The great eagle?"

"Yes, sir."

The man lowered his staff. "I am Coran, druid of the Elam Mountains." This man stared at them inquisitively. "You are awfully young to be roaming these mountains by yourself. How did you get up here?"

Toby interjected, "We were trying to get to the valley, but some troll led us the wrong direction."

"You are referring to Grud," Coran assumed.

"You know him?"

"Unfortunately, yes, and he is not to be trusted." Coran signaled for Toby to come closer. "Come over here."

Toby took several strides forward.

The druid carefully examined the details on Toby's sword. "I recognize that weapon."

Toby placed his hand on the sword's pommel.

"Only one person would possess a weapon like that." The druid bowed gracefully. "Welcome to Darnal, young Guardian. The hidden village of insurgents greets you kindly."

"Thank you." Toby offered a friendly bow. "It's a pleasure to meet all of you."

"The pleasure is ours. How did you come across the rock troll?"

"We were crossing the ruins of Moria, and he cried out for help. We helped him escape from the Hawkstrich."

Coran nodded thoughtfully. "Grud is shifty and selfish and cares only about his possessions. He remains in seclusion most of the time and will do anything to keep the Firebeast away from his hideout, including betray the tribes of Gelnoff. He is the Firebeast's pawn. If he knew the whereabouts of this place, he would be the first to reveal our location."

"Why are all of you are hiding up here?"

The goat man answered, "We hide to seek refuge from the Firebeast. He has taken everything from us and caused great upheaval in our land. He's kidnapped and killed our kin, burned down our villages, and separated us from our families. He has poured venom in the water and created burning fires that fill the country with toxic soil. He sends floods to the deserts and drought to the farmland. Lands that were once fertile are now parched. Water that was once drinkable is now poisoned. He will stop at nothing until every one of us is either imprisoned or dead."

The elf added more to the story. "Some of the bravest warriors among us stayed behind to avenge the beast and protect what's left of our land. Others came here to find solace."

"We are pleased to see you, Guardian," Coran stated. "We have heard accounts of your presence in these lands, but did not believe the tales were true. We can see now that indeed they were. If you'll come with me, we will offer you food and shelter."

"Thank you."

The youngsters in the village gave the wolf pup their full attention while Camryn and Toby followed Coran to a snow-covered hut on the opposite side of the courtyard. "That sword you possess, do you know how to use it?"

"Noraz taught me how to fight with it."

"You have befriended one of our finest," Coran said. "I'm pleased that he was able to assist you. That sword holds great power, but it is useless without the elements."

"Erramus showed me how to channel the elements."

Coran raised his eyebrows. "You saw Erramus?"

"Yes. Noraz directed us to her, and she taught me how to channel individual elements."

"You hold great power then, young Guardian. But the full force of the sword cannot be unleashed unless the elements are combined properly."

"How do I combine them?"

"It is up to you to find the right combination for each specific situation. The wrong combination can weaken the sword and he who possess it, but the right combination can make the bearer of the sword invincible."

Toby wasn't sure what that meant. He hoped that in time all of this would make sense.

Once he and Camryn dropped off their gear and situated themselves in their hut, Coran invited them to have dinner with him and the other elders. They were served hot soup and bread, and Coran poured each of them a cup of what appeared to be cranberry juice. Coran wanted to know how much Toby knew about the tribes and history of their land, so he asked, "Tell us what you know about Gelnoff."

Toby explained what he had learned so far. "I only know what I've been told. Apparently some ancient creatures called Treelings hold some kind of magical power over the land and the elements. They have the capability of binding the elements together, which maintains balance throughout Gelnoff. The Firebeast wants to take that power from them and use it for his own wicked purposes. It is my understanding that the Firebeast can't control any of the elements, with the exception of Fire. So he and the Treelings had some sort of battle to fight for possession of the other elements. To protect the elements, and keep the Firebeast from gaining control over them, the Treelings ran away. In return, the Firebeast tortured and tormented every village to try to get the tribes to reveal the Treeling's location. He set fire to everything, which polluted the water and the land. And with the Treelings gone, the elements are out of whack. Because of his selfish greed, the entire land of Gelnoff is now in disarray, and I guess the only way to fix it is to get rid of the Firebeast."

Coran bowed his head. "You know much, young one. Once the Firebeast is eliminated, the Treelings will return, the elements will reunite, and balance will return to our land."

"I get that, but there's one thing I don't understand," Toby said.

"What is that?"

"If this Firebeast is causing so many problems, why didn't all of you just form some sort of army and fight him yourselves?"

"Only the strength of the sword is effective against him. Many have spent years seeking that weapon you possess, but the sword has kept itself hidden. It only appears when in the presence of he who has the skill, agility, and mental capacity to channel the energy within the sword. One cannot simply pick up the Sword of Aonghus and draw out its power. The sword chooses you."

This didn't make things much clearer. Why, when all of these creatures were bigger, stronger, and obviously more experienced than he was, did the sword choose him? "Why me?"

"The sword saw something in you. Something no one else possesses."

"Maybe the sword was wrong."

"That sword was forged from the elements, and the elements are never wrong."

When they returned to their hut for the night, the wolf pup curled up on the ground and slept while Camryn and Toby studied the tome, gaining as much knowledge about various element combinations as they could.

"I'm never going to remember all of this," Toby said, and he leaned back onto a straw mattress. His head hurt from the overabundance of information he had received over the last few weeks.

"I'll help you. We'll review the book every night, and you can practice as we travel."

Camryn reached inside her bag to put the tome away and frantically dug around as if she'd lost something. "Where is it?"

"Where's what?"

"The key. I know I put it in here." She shifted the bag's contents multiple times and pulled items out one by one, setting them on the floor beside her. The skeleton key was gone. She pursed her lips together and drew her eyebrows forward. "The troll," she said. "He must have stolen it while we were sleeping."

Toby stared at her with an angry scowl. "Not only did he lead us down the wrong path, he also stole our stuff. Why would he steal a key?"

"I don't know. But we need to get it back. That key must be important or he wouldn't have taken it."

"He led us this way because he wanted to create a diversion to bide himself time so he could warn the Firebeast that we're coming."

"Then we need to intercept him before he can."

Chapter 10

When the sun rose in the morning, Coran gave Toby and Camryn warm clothes, a few days' worth of food and water, and a map with specific instructions to guide them in the right direction. Before they left the village, he said, "The fiery lair lies beyond the misty lake, in the valley of Gist. But beware of his feathered sentinels. They will do anything to protect the lair."

Camryn slipped the map in her pocket and threw her backpack over her shoulders. "We'll be careful."

Toby shook Coran's hand. "Thanks for your help."

"You are more than welcome. The elders and I will keep everyone safe until you return." He held his staff to his side and bowed respectfully. "Good luck, young Guardian, and safe travels."

Toby and Camryn gave one last glance behind them then bid farewell to the people of Garnal.

With the wolf leading the way, they trekked up the stairs back to the mountain path by the river. Several feet of snow blanketed the ground, and with the chill in the air, they could see their breath.

"Well, here we go again," Toby said. "Off on another adventure." Even after the training he received from Noraz and Erramus, and the conversation he had with Coran, Toby still had no idea how he was going to pull off this impossible task placed before him. He was convinced that no matter what he did, he had no chance of defeating a horrible Firebeast. "We're one step closer to the Firebeast's lair, and one step closer to my death."

Despite Toby's cynicism, Camryn found the quest they were on rather exciting. "I think you're underestimating your abilities. Noraz and Erramus gave you the tools you need, you just have to learn how to combine the elements to get the most power out of them."

"That's not as easy as you think it is, Camryn. And even if I do figure out how to combine the elements, the sword is useless without the other two stones. We have no idea where they are or even where to begin searching for them."

"There must be clues somewhere. Have you had any more visions?"

"Not since we left the temple. Maybe the visions only appear if I'm on holy ground or something."

Camryn didn't agree. "I think Erramus would have told you if that were the case. We need to think this through. We're missing something important."

As they walked along the path, leaving footprints in the snow, Toby spotted an unusual tree on a hilltop. Its metallic leaves and white branches glimmered under a bright yellow sunbeam. "That's weird. I don't remember seeing that tree before. Do you?"

"No," Camryn stated.

Toby's ring began to glow. "I think we should go up there."

Camryn agreed. "I think you're right."

They hiked up the hill to get a closer look, but the higher they climbed, the steeper the hill became. The incline on this hill made the hike to the top almost impossible. Ten minutes of hiking felt like hours, and if they stopped to rest, the distance between them and the tree grew wider.

"This hill didn't seem this steep when we started," Camryn noted. "We're not making much progress."

Although blistering wind swirled around them, piercing their skin like razors, Toby wasn't about to give up. "Something's up there. We need to keep climbing."

The ring Toby wore grew brighter with every step.

After what seemed like hours, Toby and Camryn finally reached the summit. Thick snow blanketed the ground, and freezing wind howled around them, yet the area surrounding this tree was lush and green. Despite the windy conditions, the tree's branches were undisturbed, and the leafy twigs held no snow. In fact, no snow flurries fell anywhere near this tree.

Triple spiral markings were carved into the tree's trunk, the same markings they found on one of the sacred stones by the river. Toby's ring grew brighter, and a dazzling light illuminated from the highest tree branch. He pointed it out to Camryn. "Look up there."

Camryn raised her eyes to look. "What is that?"

"I don't know, but there's only one way to find out." He dropped his sword and backpack on the ground and began to climb the tree.

"Be careful," Camryn warned.

Toby was an accomplished tree climber. He spent the majority of his childhood climbing trees. He loved the freedom nesting in the branches gave him, and often retreated to the tree fort in his backyard.

Hidden within the boughs, Toby found a glowing yellow stone about the size of a marble. He reached his hand into the limbs and gained possession of the sparkling gem.

He slipped it into his pants' pocket then made his descent back down the tree.

"What did you find?" Camryn asked.

Toby pulled the stone from his pocket and showed it to Camryn. "The third stone."

The crossguard of Toby's sword had a lion's head on each side. Each lion's mouth was open just far enough to fit a stone inside. Toby pulled the yellow stone out of his pocket and placed it in one of the lion's mouths. Instantly, the blade illuminated bright yellow. "We have three stones now," he said. "Only one more to go."

"Yup, but before we look for that one, we have to make a side stop."

Toby gathered his gear, then he and Camryn trekked back down the snow-covered hill to the path below. They retraced their steps and backtracked all the way to the troll's hideout under the bridge.

When they arrived, Toby drew his sword and tapped on the door.

Footsteps scampered from behind the wooden barricade, and it took several minutes before the troll showed his face.

Toby pointed the tip of his sword right at the troll's chest. "Alright, Grud, cough it up."

The troll flinched and stepped backward.

The wolf pup crouched, ready to pounce, and Camryn pulled her bow string. She pointed a sharp arrow tip right at Grud's throat. "Why did you steal our key?" she asked, trying to get the troll to fess up. "Give it back."

The troll cowered in fear. "Please don't hurt me. I meant no harm."

"No harm? You took something that didn't belong to you."

"I only took it because I don't want the Firebeast to come after me."

"Why would he come after you?" Toby asked. "It's come to our attention that you work for him."

The troll strongly denied this statement. "No, no, no. I merely give him what he wants, and because of that, he allows me to venture into other lands to replenish my supplies."

Toby snorted and shook his head. "You mean all this swag you stole."

"If you go after him, his fiery rage will come back to me. I will no longer be allowed access into other lands. My supplies will be depleted, and I'll be forced into slavery."

"You're his personal pickpocket, aren't you?"

"I'm merely trying to survive like everyone else in these tormented lands. As long as I offer payment, he leaves me alone."

"That's probably why the Hawkstrich held you captive. You tried to steal his stuff too, didn't you?"

"I was hungry and wanted eggs."

"You're nothing but a common thief." Toby pushed the sword blade against Grud's leathery skin. "Why did you send us the wrong way?"

"To keep you from finding the Firebeast. If he's disturbed, he'll engulf everything around him in flames, including my home."

Camryn put in her two cents' worth. "He's kidnapped children and torn families apart. He's a murderer. Look around. He's destroyed this land and disrupted the peace and balance that once flourished here. You enabled him to do this by giving him what he wants. I wouldn't be surprised if you ratted everyone out to save your own skin."

"Where's the key, Grud?" Toby demanded. "Give it back right now or you'll never see the light of day again."

The troll trembled. "Ok. Ok, just don't hurt me, please."

He retreated down the pathway with Camryn and Toby close behind him. Once they entered his living quarters, the troll reached into a clay pot and pulled out a black skeleton key with an orange crystal on it.

Camry swiped it out of his hand. "What else have you stolen from us?"

"Nothing. I swear." The troll held up his hands to surrender.

"You are the worst person, or thing, or whatever you are, I have ever met. You should be ashamed of yourself for acting so selfishly. People have died trying to protect their families and fellow tribesmen, and others are fighting back. Yet all you do is sit in your swag house, steal things of value, and use them to bribe the Firebeast. You're a coward is what you are. A selfish coward." She drew her bow again and pointed it right at him. "Toby and I are leaving, and you better not try to stop us."

"No, no. Please go. Leave me in peace."

When the troll turned away, Camryn released her bow string and shot him in the butt. Grud gripped his backside with both hands and wallowed in pain.

"Serves you right," Toby said, laughing under his breath.

They left the troll's hideout and continued their journey.

They crossed a thick mud bog into a valley. The ground felt soggy under their feet, and the land around them was fire damaged. Grass and bushes were burned, and chunks of coal lined the rocky trails. Acrid smoke and steam rose up from the ground, and the air was thick with humidity. The only remaining plant life was covered in soot.

Camryn took a whiff of the putrid air and curled her lip. "Eww. That smells awful."

"Kinda like your shoes," Toby teased.

Camryn smacked him in the arm.

"Ow!" Toby's stomach grumbled and his throat felt dry. "We need to find food soon. I'm starving."

"Good luck finding anything in this horrid place. The only creature that would live in a place like this is an ogre."

The wolf pointed his nose and sniffed at the ground, following a scent along the edge of the path. An amphibian-looking creature with a round body, webbed feet, and large, floppy hound dog ears popped out from behind a rock.

Toby pointed at it and laughed. "What is that thing?"

"How would I know?"

The creature croaked and hopped across the path to the other side. The wolf pup bounded over to the rock and four more came out of hiding, all in various sizes from about four inches long to about a foot and a half. Each was a different color, ranging from yellow to purple, and all had odd swirly patterns on their backs.

"That is the strangest creature I've ever seen."

The wolf nudged at one with his snout.

"Come on, boy," Toby said, distracting the wolf. "Leave them alone."

They continued down the path until they saw a mist-covered lake. They trudged around a pile of rocks and stopped to rest near a fallen log on the opposite shore. The water around this area was thick with tall, skinny reeds, and strange looking fish with three eyes swam in and out of the overgrown water plants. Camryn removed her backpack and held her bow in her hand. "I'm going to scout the area for food. Why don't you scavenge around and see if you can find something edible."

"Sounds good."

Utilizing the wolf pup's sense of smell, Toby foraged for edible plant life while Camryn crept around the area searching for any kind of game animal she could find. A bird with a stout body pecked at the ground. Camryn pulled an arrow from her quiver and aligned it with the bow string. She held the bow at shoulder height and took aim, pulling the string back.

"Hey, Camryn!" Toby shouted, scaring away any animal within fifty yards of them.

Camryn lowered her bow. "Really, Toby? You had to yell like that? I almost had a bird until you startled it."

"Sorry."

The wolf pup leapt into the lake and dipped his face in the water. He came back up with a slimy fish gripped between his teeth. He paddled to shore, shook the water off his fur, and munched on the juicy fish meat.

That gave Toby an idea. He leaned over and picked up a branch. "Why don't we just make a fishing pole and catch some of these fish?"

"With what fishing line?"

Toby rummaged through his pack and found a roll of thin twine. "I have this string. All we need is a hook." He searched his bag for a hook but couldn't find anything useful.

"Here," Camryn said, handing him one of her earrings. "Will this work?"

"It might." With a sharp rock and his pocketknife, he molded the earring into a U shape, forming a pointy barb on the end. He tied it onto the string then cut off an eight-foot length of twine and attached it to the branch. "There," he said, satisfied with his work. "That might do the trick."

He stepped closer to the edge of the lake and tossed the line into the water. With a few tugs and nibbles, he was able to hook a ten-inch fish. They cooked it over a campfire.

"How are we going to find the other stone?" Toby asked, hoping Camryn had the answer.

"The only one left is the Fire stone," Camryn said. "The Water stone was at the bottom of a well, and the Wind stone was in the top of a tree in the middle of a blizzard. That means the Fire stone is most likely hidden within these charred ruins."

While they ate, giant bird-like creatures hovered overhead. Toby looked to the sky to get a better view of them. They had human-like features with long, beautiful hair draped around their lovely faces. Atop their heads, they wore purple and gold plumage crowns. Purple and gold-frilled tail feathers formed a train behind them. These beautiful creatures flew majestically in the air.

When Toby looked away to take a bite of his fish, his ring illuminated bright red. "What is happening?"

With a high pitched squeal, one of these magnificent creatures swooped down from the sky and clawed at Camryn with its long, curved talons. Camryn tried to shoo the creature away, but she was quickly swarmed by a full flock of them. They yanked at her hair while they circled around her, leaving her surrounded and unable to move.

These must have been the creatures the village druid warned them about. Taking action, Toby gripped his sword with both hands and flew through the air, swinging wildly. "Stay away from my sister!"

The wolf pup joined the fight by nipping at the creatures' legs and swiping at their wings with his paw. They retaliated by clawing at him, leaving scratch marks and open wounds on his skin. Camryn, Toby, and the wolf pup put up quite a fight, yet despite their valiant efforts, the harpies captured Camryn and flew off with her, taking the tome and the key with them.

"Camryn!" Toby hollered, chasing after her. But it was no use. The winged-creatures disappeared into the horizon.

Feeling defeated, Toby fell to his knees. His heart fell to his stomach, and for a moment he couldn't breathe. "I can't do this." He dropped his sword on the ground and hung his head. "How can I defeat a Firebeast when I can't even protect my own sister?"

With a whimper, the wolf pup crouched on the ground next to Toby and slowly nudged the sword toward him.

Toby glanced down at the pup. "What?"

The pup looked him in the eye and whined.

Toby shook his head. "I can't do this alone," he said, his voice thick with doubt. "Camryn's the one who got us this far. Without her, we have no chance of making it through this alive."

The pup pushed the sword closer, encouraging Toby to carry on.

"Didn't you hear what I said?" he scolded the pup. "We can't do this without Camryn."

The wolf pup refused to give in. He scooped the sword in his mouth and stared at Toby.

Toby knew what the wolf pup wanted. He gritted his teeth, and his knuckles turned white from the fist he formed. He pounded his fist into the ground and hopped to his feet. "You're right," he said to the pup. "Come on. We're getting her back."

Toby took his sword from the pup and slid it back in the sheath. Then he picked up Camryn's bow and quiver and patted the wolf's rump.

The canine whimpered.

"You're hurt." Toby examined the wolf and discovered several gashes that left his fur matted with blood. "Let's get you cleaned up."

The wolf pup affectionately licked his hand.

Chapter 11

Toby had no idea where he was going or how he was going to get Camryn back. But trudging up a stone-covered trail to the other side of a dark, misty lake was not the time for second guessing. The air was thick. Fog hovered over the path, and water saturated the ground below him. The entire area smelled musty. Condensation formed on the blade of his sword, and his clothes were damp from the moisture in the air. Toby's feet sank into the mud, which made a sloshy, slurping sound every time he lifted his foot.

"This place is nasty. It reminds me of the Florida mud bogs."

The wolf pup sniffed the air, searching for Camryn's scent. Almost instantly, his hackles spiked upright, and his ears perked up.

"What is it, boy? What do you hear?"

The pup growled from the depths of his throat.

Toby scanned the area but didn't see anything unusual. "What do you smell? Did you find Camryn?"

The wolf darted toward the lake's edge. Toby chased after him.

On the other side of the path, Toby discovered a hidden cave. "What's in there?"

The wolf lowered his front paws closer to the ground and belly crawled toward the entrance. He sniffed at the soil. With his tail pointed out and nose pointed forward, he whimpered.

"She's in there, isn't she?" Toby squinted to get a better look, but it was so dark inside the enclosure that he couldn't see anything. "Come on. Let's get her back."

They made their way through the rocky entrance. The area inside the cave smelled like decaying garbage and sulfur. Water dripped from the roof of an enormous cavern, echoing with a *plip plop* every time a droplet fell into the pool below.

"It's dark and dank in here." The air inside the cave became more stagnant. Toby curled his lip. "And it smells like rotten fish."

He couldn't tell where they were going because their only light source came from the glow of his ring.

"Where is she, boy? Where's Camryn?"

A squealing noise from deep within the cave walls quickly drew their attention to a passageway on the left. Light flickered in the distance. "If she is in here, we need to hurry and get her out."

Toby and the wolf pup slunk down this passageway. Smoke drifted across the cave floor, and the squeals became louder. Trying to stay hidden, Toby peeked around a protruding rock structure. A flock of harpies stood in a circle, flapping their wings and squawking. Camryn was right in the middle of them, trapped in a six-foot pit in the center of the room. With his hand on the pommel of his sword, Toby drew back, sighing. "How are we going to get her out of here?"

The wolf pup cocked his head.

Toby hoped the animal had some ingenious plan and could somehow communicate this with him. No such luck. He was on his own.

"We need to create a distraction so I can get down there."

The wolf knew what that meant. Slipping away from Toby's side, the pup ran into the room and whisked right past the harpies, howling at the top of his lungs. A dozen or so squealing, squawking harpies chased after him, leaving only one in the room with Camryn.

"Clever." Toby drew his sword and snuck up behind the remaining harpy. The tip of the blade jabbed into the back of her neck. "Don't move," he said.

With a high-pitched squeal, the harpy swung around and swatted Toby with her wing. It knocked him off his feet.

"Toby!" Camryn called to him. "Toss me my bow!"

The harpy charged at him with bloodshot eyes; her sharp talons spread open. Toby gripped his sword with both hands and swung at the base of her wing. It cut clean through.

Screaming bloody murder, the harpy withdrew long enough for Toby to stand up and toss Camryn's bow and quiver into the pit. "I don't know how long I can hold her off!" he told his sister, prepared to fight this angry bird woman to the death to save Camryn.

With one wing severely injured, the harpy was unable to fly. She cleverly used her remaining wing as a weapon and tried to knock Toby into the pit with Camryn. She almost connected several times.

"Get her to follow you to the edge so I can get a good shot at her," Camryn advised.

Dodging wing strikes and counterattacking any chance he could, Toby darted from one side of the room to the other. "I am not standing anywhere near that pit. She'll knock me down there with you then we'll both be trapped." Instead, he ran around in circles around the room, dodging to his left and right, trying to disorient the wounded beast and wear her down.

Camryn placed an arrow in her bow and pulled the string back, taking aim at the moving target. But every time she had a clear shot, Toby blocked the way. "Move," she said to him. "I can't get a shot with you standing in front of her."

Toby evaded the harpy's strike and ducked to the right again. "What do you want me to do, Camryn? This thing is trying to kill me." He took another strike at the harpy and sliced through the tip of her other wing.

She squealed and fell backwards, which finally gave Camryn a chance to strike. With a snap of her bow string, she released the arrow. It was a clear shot, straight through the harpy's chest. The harpy gasped for air and collapsed to the cave floor.

The cavern fell eerily silent.

Toby lowered his sword and panted to catch his breath.

"Get me out of this pit," Camryn's voice echoed through the room. "It won't be long before the others come back."

Toby returned his sword to its proper place then reached into his pack and pulled out a coil of rope. He unrolled it and tossed the end to Camryn. "I'll loop the other end around this big rock, but you're going to have to pull yourself up." He used a nearby boulder as leverage and gripped the other end tightly in his hands. "Ok. Pull yourself up, but you need to hurry."

Camryn threw the quiver on her back and attached the bow to the outside. She then gripped the rope with both hands and climbed up the wall. As soon as her feet touched the cave floor, she and Toby rushed down the nearest corridor, hoping it led to an exit.

As they searched passageways for a way out, etchings of flames, spirals, and interconnected circles appeared on the cave walls. A bright red light lit up a nearby hallway, and a low hum resonated through the cavern. "There's something over there." Toby followed the sound, which led him to a narrow corridor. As he approached the light, his ring gleamed brighter. He followed the light further down the tunnel. Around the corner, directly in the center of a small chamber, a bright red gem hovered over a pedestal.

Toby's eyes widened. "Whoa!"

Camryn bolted around the corner and almost bumped into him. "Don't run off like that. I…" When she saw Toby in the middle of this room with his mouth gaped open, she knew right away what he was staring at. "There it is. The elemental Fire stone."

He slowly inched toward the pedestal and reached for the stone, but a powerful force field repelled his effort. "What the…" He reached for the stone again, but every time he tried to grab it, a mysterious barrier pushed his hand away. "Does it say anything in that book about a hidden force field surrounding this stone?"

Camryn flipped through the pages, scanning every section for clues. Nothing was written about a floating stone. "I can't find anything," she said, feeling Toby's frustration. "All it says is that the Fire stone is full of energy and can lead to uncontrollable rage if not contained. It doesn't say anything about a stone hidden beneath a barrier."

"There has to be a way to retrieve this stone." He threw a large rock at the levitating gem, but all it did was bounce back at him. He tried poking it with a stick, but that didn't work either. He and Camryn searched the entire room for a hidden lever or switch that might release the force field. They found nothing.

Discouraged, Toby bashed the pommel of his sword against the invisible barrier. All three stones on his sword lit up, and the levitating crystal glowed furiously. A crimson light pulsated several times before the pedestal cracked and crumbled to the ground. The red gem fell with it. The Fire stone rolled across the floor and came to a stop near the chamber entrance. Toby's sword returned to normal, his ring stopped glowing, and the humming sound faded.

He picked up the stone and stared at it for a moment before he slid it into the lion's mouth on the sword's crossguard. "There," he said as he placed the sword back in its sheath. "Now let's get out of here."

Camryn and Toby twisted and turned through multiple corridors, unable to locate an exit. Long, dark pathways led to even darker corridors. Squealing harpies shrieked behind them, quickly closing in.

They hit several dead ends and had to turn around multiple times only to encounter another empty pocket with no way out.

"We're never going to get out of here," Toby complained.

Camryn hoped to jog his memory. "Which way did you come in?"

"I don't remember." The chamber they were in had three pathways. One led to the left, one to the right, and the other straight ahead of them. Toby looked to the left. "Let's go this way."

The wolf appeared from the passage in front of them and stood on alert. He pointed his nose in the air, sniffed the wind, then darted down the corridor on the right.

"I think we should go that way," Camryn countered, following the wolf's natural instincts.

"I think you're right."

They followed the wolf through the cave depths until they encountered a beam of light at the end of a tunnel. They raced toward the exit, which led them outside, right at the base of a rocky ravine. Toby leaned on his knees to catch his breath.

"We can't stop now," Camryn insisted. "In case you forgot, harpies are chasing us. We need to get as far away from here as we can."

"We've been running forever. I…" A screaming harpy stormed out of the cave and swooped down at Toby. Toby drew his sword and swung at her, connecting with the flesh of her leg.

She dove at him again, squawking furiously with fiery, red eyes. Her sharp talons scraped across his skin, tearing at his shirt sleeve and leaving him with an open wound.

"Oh yeah? You wanna play rough?" Blood oozed from his shoulder, but Toby firmly stood his ground. He gripped the sword with both hands and cried, "Alright, you evil cretin! You're going down!"

Rage brewed in Toby's eyes, and the blade of his sword turned bright red. The crystal embedded within the lion's mouth beamed, giving everything nearby a ruddy hue. Without hesitation, Toby swung his sword around and charged at the winged beast in a frenzied barrage, aiming the blade right at her chest. The metal scraped against her rib cage, grinding at the edges of the blade. The harpy squealed in agony and fell to the ground. She flapped her wings violently and kicked her legs to fight Toby off.

Toby refused to give in. He pulled the sword from her chest, hollered into the air, and struck her again, killing her on impact.

Camryn couldn't believe what she witnessed from her brother. The spontaneity of his actions and the fury in his eyes—she had never seen him exude that much rage. Only the power of Fire would have given him that kind of ferocity.

The Fire element was known to be forceful, bold, and energetic, but Fire was also combustible. If left unattended, Fire burned out of control. Camryn had to intervene before her brother's rage blinded him. "Toby," she called to him, using her voice to soothe and talk him out of the trance he was in. "Toby, look at me."

Toby's bloodshot eyes drifted to Camryn. His pupils were dark red, and his hands were cold and clammy.

"Breathe, Toby. Just calm down."

He pulled the blade from the harpy's chest and loosened his grip on the sword. It fell to the ground. Toby's knees buckled from underneath him, and he collapsed to the rocky surface below.

Camryn rushed to his side. "Are you alright?"

"I can't…" He struggled to regain oxygen. "I can't breathe."

"Take deep breaths." She wrapped her arm around his shoulder and helped him rise to his feet. "Let's get you out of here. Come on."

She gathered the rest of their belongings and directed Toby to a trail just offshore.

Chapter 12

The trail wound around a rocky ravine into a forest flattened by fire. Steam and smoke rose from the surface of the land, and the entire area was covered in charcoal and soot.

"We need to take care of that wound on your shoulder," Camryn told her brother when his shirt sleeve became blood-soaked. "The last thing we need is for you to develop an infection."

They made camp under a rocky overhang then Camryn doctored Toby's wound. While he rested, she gathered charred wood chips, a few loose branches, and whatever sticks she could find. With Toby's guidance, she used a flint stone to start a campfire. She rationed out some water and dried meat for them and the wolf, then she pulled the tome from her bag and read by firelight.

"According to legend, the elemental key unlocks the heart of Gelnoff, but only the Guardian is allowed to cross the barrier." She pulled the black skeleton key from her bag and stared at it. "Suppose the legend is talking about this key?"

"I guess." Toby shrugged. "That's the only key we've found."

"It says here that a secret archway appears. It's sealed by a gate. The Guardian in the only one who can unlock it."

"What kind of archway? Is there a picture of it in there?"

Camryn flipped through the pages. "No. But it does say that the Firebeast's lair lies within the heart of Gelnoff."

"So I have to get through this secret barrier to get to him?"

"That's what it sounds like. The instructions aren't very clear here."

Toby leaned back and sighed. "Great. Not only do I have to fight this Firebeast, I also have to unlock some kind of secret door just to get to him. Whoever came up with this ingenious plan sure didn't make it very easy, did they? From the second we arrived in this place, we've encountered one problem after another. I'm tired, and I would give anything for a cheeseburger right now."

Camryn laughed at Toby's suggestion. "I would too."

Toby fluffed his backpack a few times and tried to get comfortable. "I miss my bed."

Camryn leaned back and stared up at the stars. Images of her parents flowed through her mind, which brought tears to her eyes. "Dad would have enjoyed this adventure."

"He would have." Toby remembered all the times he and his father went camping and fishing together. The two of them spent every weekend outdoors enjoying nature. Toby would have given anything to have just one more day with his father. "I've never known anyone who could do so much with so little. All Dad needed was a few branches, a roll of twine, and a pocket knife, and he could create anything. He made a fishing pole, tent stakes, and even built an entire shelter from the things he carried in his backpack." Toby's eyes welled with tears. The thought of continuing through life without his parents tugged at his heart. "I wish Dad was here right now. He would have found a way to get us out of this."

Throughout the night, Camryn and Toby reminisced about all the fun times they shared with their parents. The conversation brought about many emotions, but it was also a bonding experience for them. Through the conversation, they both realized that they would have to rely on each other more than ever if they were going to make it through this alive.

In the morning, they continued their journey. Several miles up the road, they ran into a single green plant. "Hmm. That's odd," Camryn said. "Everything around here is burned beyond recognition except for this plant."

This plant had semi-woody stems with small wispy fronds. Each frond had hundreds of long, narrow leaves that grew from the base of the frond all the way up to the tip of the plant. Each leaf had spores on the back. A long tendril grew from one of the fronds and clung to a nearby rock.

"What a weird looking plant," Camryn said, examining the details of the leaves. This plant looked a lot like a fern, except it was much larger than any fern she had ever seen before, and it was growing in a dry environment, something ferns didn't do. "How is it staying alive out here?"

"How does anything stay alive out here?" Toby added. "This place is miserable."

When Camryn leaned in to get a more detailed look at one of the leaves, a man in a hooded cloak popped out from the center of the plant, startling her. She placed her hand on her pounding heart and stared at him. "You scared the heck out of me."

"My apologies. I did not mean to frighten you."

She lifted the fronds and looked around all sides of the plant. "Where did you come from?"

"My name is Perth. I am the druid of Gist. What are you doing in these lands?"

"We're looking for the Firebeast's lair."

"Why?"

Toby stepped forward with his hand on the pommel of his sword. "We were sent here by Erramus."

The druid's eyes widened. "You've spoken to her?"

"Yes. She invited me into her temple and taught me how to channel the elements."

Perth examined the sword in Toby's hand. "That's the elemental sword of Aonghus."

Toby nodded.

The druid bowed respectfully. "Welcome to the Valley of Gist, young Guardian. We have anticipated your arrival for quite some time."

"So I've heard."

The druid sat on a nearby stump and pointed off to the distant horizon. "The Firebeast's lair hides deep within the black cliffs of Gelnoff, where an underground river flows. Follow the smoke-filled paths to the opposite side of Misty Lake. There, you will find a gateway that can only be opened by the one who holds the key. Once the great barrier is crossed, you cannot return until the Firebeast is destroyed."

Toby released a heavy sigh. "So it's all or nothing, huh? Kill or be killed. I don't like this deal."

"The sword has chosen you, which means you are the only one who has the strength and knowledge to accomplish this task. If the sword didn't see greatness in you, it wouldn't have chosen you."

Toby snorted cynically. "What if the sword is wrong?"

"The sword is never wrong."

Toby pulled his sword from the sheath and pointed it at the druid. "What if I destroy you instead?"

Calmly, the druid turned his eyes to the tip of the blade. "The Fire element has taken control and produced much anger in you. You must learn to release the negative energy and channel the strength and wisdom within the elements. I can help you do that."

"How can you help me? You're a creepy little man who came from a bush."

The druid crossed his legs and rested his wrists on his knees. He closed his eyes and raised his chin to the wind, tuning out everything around him.

"What are you doing?" Toby asked. "Stop doing that."

Camryn stepped between Toby and the druid, forcing Toby to back off. "He's meditating," she told him. "Leave him alone."

"He's just a crazy old man. What does he know?" With the tip of his sword, Toby began stabbing at the ground.

"Why are you so angry?"

"You heard what he said. I'm never going to get out of here alive. The second I step through that barrier, I'm as good as dead."

"No, he said the only way out was to defeat the Firebeast. You make it sound like a hopeless task."

"It is a hopeless task, Camryn. Even Noraz said that he can't defeat this beast, and he's bigger and stronger than I am. I say we find a way out of here and forget about this stupid quest." Toby took off his armor and belt and threw them on the ground along with his sword. In a fit of rage, Toby kicked the charred dirt, hurling a rock through the air. "I'm tired of this place. I'm getting out of here, whether you come with me or not."

"Where are you going to go?"

"Anywhere but here."

As Toby headed down the path, the druid uttered the words, "The only way out is through."

Toby swung his body around and charged after the druid, grabbing him by the throat. "I'm tired of people saying that to me!" His bloodshot eyes turned fiery red, and his knuckles turned white with rage. He was paralyzed by illogical hatred. "I don't like you, I don't trust you, and I'm not listening to you."

Camryn tried to pry Toby's hand off the druid's neck. "Let go of him. What is wrong with you?"

His grip grew tighter, and the fury in his eyes pierced through the druid like a dagger.

"Toby, let go," Camryn insisted.

Within seconds, the overwhelming power of anger drained from Toby's body and he fell to the ground, sweating profusely.

Camryn looked over at the druid, who appeared unaffected by this episode. "What just happened?" she asked, hoping the druid had answers for her.

"The Fire element has consumed him."

Camryn peered over at her brother, who was now curled up in a ball, shivering. "Why is he shaking like that?"

"The Fire element is powerful. If left uncontrolled, anger, fear, and hatred will overpower the mind. It can bring even the kindest person into an uncontrollable fit of rage. Fear and uncertainty provide fuel for Fire, which lead to anger. This anger depletes all energy and leaves you unable to think clearly."

"Can he learn to control it?"

"He *must* learn to control it. Giving in to the impulses of anger is a sign of weakness, and the Firebeast will use that to his advantage. Through meditation, your brother can learn to discharge the negative energy and channel the power of Fire without giving in to anger."

"Can you show him how?"

"I can, if he is willing to accept help. But he must request the help himself."

While Camryn and the druid conversed, Toby's mind drifted in and out of consciousness. Images of his father flooded his head. He drifted off to the faint sound of someone calling his name. "Toby."

Toby squinted his eyes, trying to clear the voice from his head.

"Why do you doubt your abilities? You've always been resourceful," the voice said to him. "You know the wilderness well. You grew up outdoors. Use what you know. You are well prepared, and you can do this."

Toby groaned and rolled onto this side.

"Let go of the conscious world as you know it and use your knowledge to your advantage. Utilize your strengths."

"I can't. I…"

"I believe in you, son, but you must believe in yourself."

The image slowly drifted from Toby's mind. With his knees clenched into his chest, he regained consciousness and opened his eyes. Dazed and confused, he sat up. "Where am I?"

The druid cleared his throat. "You are in the valley of Gist."

Toby scanned his surroundings, trying to orient himself. "Where's my sister?"

Camryn sat beside him and placed her hand on his back. "I'm right here. You fell into some kind of trance and collapsed."

"I did?"

"Yes. Apparently the Fire element is so powerful, it took control over you."

Toby raised his hand to his forehead. "I don't remember any of that. My mind just went blank."

"Anger affects your thinking," the druid explained. "It can cloud your vision, which can make you impulsive and reactionary. In a fight, that can be deadly."

Toby stared at the red stone on his sword. How could such a tiny rock have so much power? "What is the Fire element doing to me?"

"It is not the element that controls your emotions, it is you. No one other than yourself has the power to make you angry. Anger is something that's created in your own mind. You must discharge this negative energy and learn to relax."

"How?"

"Do not deny anger. Turn toward your anger rather than fighting against it. Anger converts to energy. Allow this energy to spread all over your body and create peacefulness."

"How is that even possible?"

"Take a few deep breaths. Synchronize the mind with every breath, thus increasing your energy levels and calming your body. When the mind is calm and quiet, agitation is less likely. This peacefulness will make you feel more alive and vibrant."

Toby breathed in deeply and exhaled. With every breath, he felt the angry tension fade from his body and a cool sensation skim over his skin.

"Good. Now close your eyes," the druid instructed.

Toby did as he was told.

"Use your imagination, picture yourself lying on the beach, walking in the forest, floating on a cloud, or leaning against a tree next to a serene lake, whatever scene you associate with relaxation. Live it. Be in the moment. Use every sense to pull your body into the scene."

Toby's mind cleared, and he felt like he was sinking into a pool of water. Energy surged through his body, and he suddenly felt invincible. Fatigue began to fade, and hunger pangs in his stomach subsided. His visions became clearer. It wasn't long before a wave of energy from Water, Air, and Earth filled his body and drowned out the overwhelming power of Fire.

"Now, remember that feeling. Every time you feel anger, sink into your visions. Pull in the energy from all the elements. Relax. Clear your mind, and let the energy flow through you."

Once Toby was calm, he re-strapped his armor to his chest and reattached his belt to his waist. He placed his sword in its sheath and threw his pack on his back. "Which way do we go?"

The druid bowed his head. "Follow the shores of the misty lake to the great barrier line. The black tower conceals the gate, hidden in a path of vines."

"How will we know when we've reached the barrier?" When Toby turned his head, the druid and fern were gone. Only the charred remains of a plant remained. "Well, I guess we're on our own again."

Camryn readjusted her gear and took a few strides forward. "We need to keep moving."

"Camryn," Toby called to his sister. "I saw Dad."

She stopped dead in her tracks. "You couldn't have seen Dad, Toby. He's gone."

"I saw him in my vision, when I was on the ground. He spoke to me."

Camryn didn't believe him. "He spoke to you?"

"Yes. He reached his hand out to me and told me he believed in me."

She whipped around and looked him in the eye. "Wait a minute, you can see Dad in your visions?"

"I've never been able to before, but this time, I did."

"What else did he say?"

"He told me to utilize my strengths and use what I know. I saw his face, Camryn. He was standing right in front of me."

Camryn gripped at her heart and had to fight to retain her composure. "Come on." She smiled at her younger brother. "We have to keep going."

With a heavy sigh, Toby followed Camryn down the dirt road.

Chapter 13

A smoky mist rose from the gravel-covered path, and eerie black clouds swirled around in the sky overhead, the same black clouds they first encountered when they crossed the waterfall barrier into the dark forest. The landscape was full of row upon row of eroded black limestone, which produced sharp, pointy towers that seemed to go on forever. The scene was quite beautiful, especially with the lake in the foreground.

"This isn't so bad," Camryn commented. "It kind of looks like Rose Lake back home."

They traversed up the rocky path to an ancient stone archway covered in thorny vines. As Toby approached the archway, it glowed crimson red. Toby's ring illuminated with it. A keyhole appeared on the gateway, along with the words *Only the Guardian may enter here.* "This looks like the right place."

Camryn inserted the key, but the lock would not budge. "Maybe we have the wrong key."

A red mist rose from the keyhole, and a mystical voice whispered, "Kia-lekota raktas."

Toby raised his eyebrows. "Hold on a minute. I've heard that phrase before."

The chant became louder and clearer. "Kia-lekota raktas."

"The amethyst stone, where we originally found the key, chanted that exact same thing. Remember?" Toby recalled.

"You're right. I do remember."

Toby held out his hand. "Give me the key."

Camryn handed it to him, and he inserted it into the lock. As he turned the key, the mystical voice repeated, "Kia-lekota raktas."

Toby recited the words, and the gateway opened.

Before he stepped inside the gate, Camryn grabbed his arm and pulled him back.

"It'll be ok," he assured her. "This is my burden, my battle to fight. Let me do this."

In haste, she called out, "I love you, Toby."

Toby gripped the handle of his sword. "Don't, Camryn. I'll be alright."

"Please be careful. Remember everything you've been taught."

He flashed her a half-hearted grin. "See you on the other side."

He entered the gateway with his sword drawn and the wolf pup at his feet. Once inside the barrier, the gate closed behind him. "This was a great idea," he snorted derisively. "No turning back now."

The wolf pup rubbed against his hand.

"It's just you and me now, buddy." He patted the wolf on the rump. "Better get moving."

He was on his own, left to pursue the Firebeast with nothing but his pack, his sword, and his trusty canine companion by his side. He didn't know where he was going or what he was facing, but he did know that the only way out of this was to do what he was brought here to do —defeat the Firebeast.

The lair was dark and smelled like charred flesh. Sharp, jagged limestone made the passage treacherous. Toby had to dodge deep crevices and endless pits to get through the dangerous entryway. "It's dark in here. How am I supposed to see where I'm going?" Each step loosened the bedrock under his feet. His foot slipped through a sinkhole and he had to fight to keep himself from falling through the crack.

A few feet into the lair, the air grew warmer, and the blade of his sword began to glow, illuminating the path in front of him. "Ok, that solved the light problem." The trail broke into a V, with no indication as to which path Toby should follow. "Which leads us to our next predicament. Which way do we go?"

It was eerily quiet. Too quiet. Toby's footprints and the padding of the wolf's paws bounced off the cave walls. No other sound was heard. The wolf sniffed the air. After careful consideration, he opted for the passage on the right. Toby followed him.

A screaming harpy, flying straight at Toby with her talons spread apart, quickly blocked their path. Instinctively, Toby bludgeoned the harpy with his sword, knocking her unconscious. He paused briefly to take stock of the situation and scan the lair. Two more harpies were on the opposite end of the passage, staring him down and baring their teeth at him. The wolf pup cornered one of them while the other one flew directly toward Toby, screaming.

He dodged her attack then swung around and slashed at her. The blade connected with a stinging blow. Her wings buckled, and she tumbled to the ground. Before she could regain her senses, Toby stood over her and ran the blade of his sword through her chest. The harpy gasped and twitched until her last breath left her.

He pulled the sword free and went after the other one, who was violently slashing at the wolf pup. She flailed her legs, trying to get away from the vicious canine, but no amount of wailing called him off. The wolf gripped her neck with his sharp teeth and bit down. With this harpy clearly under control, Toby ran back over the one he had bludgeoned, who was beginning to regain consciousness. Before she fully awoke, Toby lifted the sword above his head and cleanly decapitated her.

With the harpies now gone, Toby turned his attention to the wolf, whose muzzle was blood-soaked. "Good boy," he said to the wolf. "Now we need to find the Firebeast. Come on."

With his sword still drawn, Toby and the wolf pup followed the passageway to a dully-lit corridor. Smoke permeated the air, and steam clouded his vision.

On the far end of the corridor, a monstrous fire-breathing hybrid with a lion's head, goat's body, and a snake-head tail spotted Toby. The grotesque beast looked him straight in the eye and roared fiercely, then snorted out a raging breath of terrible flame and stood in a pounce position, ready to attack.

Toby gripped the handle of his sword with both hands and braced himself for the fight.

Load roaring and spewing smoke from the gateway left Camryn in a state of panic. She screamed Toby's name and tried to rush in after him, but the barrier held her back.

"Have faith, weary traveler." An odd-looking, furry creature with pixie wings peeked out from behind the archway.

"Who said that?"

"I did," the furry creature said. This was one of the same creatures she and Toby had seen when they first entered this land. Several more of them appeared from behind the rocks, surrounding her on all sides. "We are the Treelings."

"Treelings? You mean you're the ones who…"

"Yes," the creature interjected. "We've been communicating with you through the ring and sent you messages through the tome. We are the ones who hid the elemental stones throughout the land of Gelnoff. We forged the sword of Aonghus, and we sent the druids to guide you on your journey. Brave warriors, like Noraz and Erramus, chose to train you along the way."

"You sent them?"

"No. They volunteered their services."

Camryn tried to wrap her head around this, but with her brother in harm's way, she had a hard time comprehending exactly what was happening. "My brother…can you help him? Please, you must help him."

"Fear not," the Treeling said. "The Guardian will use his knowledge of the elements to defeat the Firebeast. He has more power than he realizes."

The wolf pup charged after the beast and was immediately slashed in the eye. He yelped, and the Firebeast threw him against the wall. The pup fell to the ground, lifeless.

"No!" Toby screamed. With adrenaline careening through his veins, he slipped into feral mode and sliced at the beast, aiming for vulnerable areas. The Firebeast shot flames at him. He ducked and dodged the beast's attack, taking refuge behind large boulders.

The Firebeast roared and charged again. He gnashed at Toby's leg and left him with a gaping wound. Toby retaliated by striking the Firebeast's hindquarters, breaking skin, which only seemed to anger the beast further.

Trying to escape, Toby gained the high ground by climbing his way up to a rocky ledge. The beast gnashed at him with his sharp claws and scratched at the ledge, leaving deep gouges in the limestone. The snake head struck, barely missing Toby's thigh. Toby swung at the serpent, penetrating through its thick skin. The snake hissed with its slithering tongue then struck again. Toby picked up a nearby rock and chucked it at the snake head, striking it right between the eyes.

In a fury, the Firebeast hammered at the rocks, knocking stones loose.

The ledge crumbled apart, and Toby had nowhere to go. Seeking guidance, he closed his eyes. Images of fishing and camping with his father filled his mind. He visualized green grass, blue skies, light breezes, and the warm sun. Although the beast roared and hacked away at him, Toby remained focused. Green, blue, yellow, and red light wisped around him. He channeled every element, taking in the endurance and strength of Earth, the thoughtfulness of Air, the energy of Fire, and the natural instinct of Water. With all four elements pouring into his soul, the sword illuminated bright white, along with the ring on Toby's hand. Energy surged, and a warm sensation flowed through his blood. His subconscious took over, and without a second thought, Toby raised the sword high above his head. He leapt off the rocky boulder and flew through the air.

The sword jabbed deep between the Firebeast's shoulder blades. The beast slashed its tail and wailed with a high-pitched roar. Toby held on, gripping the handle of the sword while the Firebeast whipped his body from side to side. With its final breath, the flames subsided and smoke bellowed from the Firebeast's mouth. His limp body tumbled to the ground, taking Toby down with him.

Chapter 14

The dark clouds disappeared and the gateway opened. With the barrier now unlocked, Camryn bolted inside the lair, hoping to find her brother alive. Harpy corpses were scattered all over the floor, and the entire lair smelled of burning flesh and wood. "Toby, where are you?" Her voice echoed off the cavern walls. "Please answer me."

No response.

She ran down another corridor, following a path of dead harpies. At the far end of a passageway, near the lifeless body of the Firebeast, Toby lay on the ground with his face buried in the ash-covered dirt. His sword lie on the ground next to him. Camryn rushed to his side. She cradled his body in her arms and propped his head on her lap. "Toby?"

He was still breathing, so she pulled her flask from her bag and forced him to sip. "Wake up," she said, and she gave him another drink.

Toby opened his eyes. "Did I kill him?" his weak voice muttered.

She held him against her chest and laughed. "Yes. You certainly did."

He turned his head to the Firebeast's dead body. With a swirl of yellow light, the remains floated away like ash in the wind.

Toby sighed in relief then took another drink. The water had a restorative effect on him, which made his wounds heal on their own. Gradually, he regained his strength.

The wolf pup's body was sprawled out, motionless on the ground. Toby stood up and ran to his furry friend's aid. He held the pup in his arms, but the wolf didn't move or make a sound. His body hung limp, unresponsive. "No," Toby wailed. "Wake up. Please wake up."

Camryn placed her hand on Toby's shoulder, trying to ease his pain.

"He tried to protect me," Toby cried. "He sacrificed himself for me."

"He was a loyal friend," she replied. "Let him rest in peace, now."

Toby wiped his eyes and gently laid the wolf's head on the ground. He patted him on the rump and slowly rose to his feet.

Camryn offered her brother a hug. "Come on. Let's get out of here."

Toby retrieved his sword, then he and Camryn followed a corridor to the exit.

On their way out, voices resounded from a nearby passageway. "What is that?" Camryn asked. "And where is it coming from?"

"It's coming from down here." Toby used the power of the Fire element to light up the dark hallway.

At the end of the hall, various species of children—Minotaurs, elves, human figures with ram's horns, goat-headed boys and girls with antlers—were all huddled together in a corner of a large pit covered with iron bars. "The missing children," Camryn exclaimed. "We found them."

One of the Minotaur children looked up. "Are you the Guardian?"

With a huge smile, Toby nodded. "Yes I am."

"My father told me about you. He said you would come."

Toby knelt down to their level. "We're going to get you out of here."

"How?"

Toby pulled his sword out and held it vertically in front of him. He closed his eyes and channeled the power of Fire. Waves of red light entered his body, which made his sword glow bright red. With one strike, the heat from the sword's blade melted the iron lock and released the iron bars. One by one, the children helped each other crawl out of their entrapment until all of them were free.

The captive children, along with Toby and Camryn, were greeted by a furry green creature about three-feet high. It had floppy jackrabbit ears, long, skinny arms and legs, and oversized toes. "Brave Guardian," the creature bowed. "You have done well. You saved our children and restored balance to this land."

The sky was now bright blue, brightening up the atmosphere. Smoke from the landscape began to clear and the dead plants unwithered. Ash that covered the ground drifted away with the breeze.

The creature spread his arms out, pointing his palms toward the sunlit sky. "Because of you, the power of Water, Earth, and Air has been released and the elements have reunited. Life has been restored to this land, and we can finally come out of hiding. Our duties as caretakers of the elements can resume."

Toby cocked his head, "Wait a minute, you're a Treeling?"

"Yes. One of the Treelings of Alderwood."

"Are you serious?" He stared at the sword in his hand, wondering how these tiny creatures had the power and ability to construct such a powerful weapon. "How did you…"

Before Toby finished his sentence, the sword glowed bright purple and all four elemental gems fell to the ground.

The Treeling grabbed the stones and carefully stuffed them in his satchel. "The elements will be returned to their proper place, but the sword, you may keep. It is our gift to you for restoring balance to Gelnoff."

"Thank you."

"I must return now." The Treeling bowed. "Thank you, Guardian. We are forever in your debt." With a swirl of white light, the Treeling disappeared.

Toby shook his head. "People sure do come and go quickly around here. How do we find our way out?"

"Aakesh," the young Minotaur suggested.

"Aakesh?"

"Yes. The mighty eagle. He can take you where you need to go."

"The eagle." Camryn remembered the large bird they saved from the frozen river. "He said all we had to do was summon him and he'd come to our aid, remember?"

"I remember," Toby said. "But how does this Minotaur know that?"

The Minotaur grinned. "Aakesh is my father's friend. Both he and my father stayed behind to help protect the land from the Firebeast."

"Your father?" Toby asked.

"Yes. I am Lunn, son of Noraz."

Both Toby and Camryn gasped. "Noraz is your father?"

"Yes, and after many years of imprisonment, I can now return to him." Lunn offered Toby a firm handshake. "Thank you, Guardian, for setting us free."

"You're welcome."

Lunn adjusted his raggedly loin cloth and headed up the stone-covered path.

Toby smiled at Camryn. "Noraz is going to be happy to see him."

"Yes he will. Now let's get out of here."

Camryn summoned the eagle by calling his name. Within minutes, he hovered overhead, squealing, before he landed at their feet. "Young Guardian. I see you have defeated the Firebeast."

"Yes, I have."

"Well done." Aakesh bowed. "How may I be of service to you?"

"Can you take us back to the hidden oasis where the Treelings hide?"

"The recluse in the forest?"

"Yes."

"As you wish." The creature crouched down and allowed Camryn and Toby to climb onto his back.

He flew them to the village where the entire clan of Treelings greeted them warmly. "Welcome back, Guardian," one of the Treelings said. "The great master would like to speak with you."

They followed a plank bridge to the other side of the river then hiked up a ramp to a wooden platform. A giant tree, with an enormous nose and mouth, opened its large, blue eyes. "Toby! You have returned to us," the tree spoke in a deep, gravelly voice. "The sword of Aonghus found you."

Toby glanced down at the sword by his side. "Yes."

"As did the messenger we sent to deliver the tome to you."

"Messenger?"

"Yes. We sent Tyree, Coran, and Perth to keep an eye on you and guide you on your journey. Thanks to them, and to you, the Treelings can now reclaim Alderwood and restore peace to this land." The tree's eyes drifted to the tribe of Treelings. "Are you ready to return home, my friends?"

"Yes," the Treelings chanted.

"Give me the gems."

The tiny Treeling took the four gemstones from his satchel and strategically placed them in four divots around the tree's face. The giant tree closed his eyes and the ground around them shook. The waterfall barrier dried up, the rocky retaining wall crumbled, and the river flowed freely through the forest, bringing life to the charred remains. The Treelings bowed gratefully then dispersed to their homeland to bring balance back to Gelnoff.

The rock staircase Toby and Camryn climbed down to get into this village reappeared on the cliff wall. The giant tree said, "Your work here is done, my friends. Your bravery will go down in history, and we will forever be grateful for your service." The tree pointed its branch toward the staircase. "You must return to your homeland now. I can only hold the exit open for a short time."

Camryn and Toby climbed up the stairs, but they gave one last glance over their shoulders to eye the Treeling village before the staircase disappeared behind them.

Chapter 15

Attached to the shapeshifter rock where Toby initially discovered the rings, they found an envelope with their names printed on it and an arrow poked through it. Camryn pulled the arrow from the rock and unfolded the note inside.

Camryn and Toby,

We're so sorry to have put you through this, but because of you, peace and harmony has been restored to Gelnoff. Thank you for your bravery and for standing by each other throughout this journey. Your father and I are very proud of you.

During the elemental wars, your father and I were the last surviving human children left in Gelnoff. All others were killed by the Firebeast. The Treelings took us in and raised us until we were old enough to marry. When the time was right, they forged wedding rings from the elements. These rings had powers to not only bring us back to the land of Gelnoff, but also to communicate with them. They sent us out to safety and instructed us train our own children to return to Gelnoff and defeat the Firebeast.

Camryn, we sent you to school for multi-lingual training as a precursor to prepare you for this quest. Your ability to read and speak in many languages allowed you to translate the inscriptions on the stones and read the book of elements. Toby, we put you in Boy Scouts to learn survival skills. Your father taught you how to start a campfire, build a shelter, and forage for food in preparation for this journey. Once you were trained, the only way to get you to Gelnoff was for us to die and pass the rings on to you.

Noraz the Minotaur, in hopes of saving his children from enslavement, volunteered to create a diversion. He jumped in front of the car and blocked the road, which caused the vehicle to spin out of control. From there, the plan fell into place. The rings were strategically placed where you would find them, and the Treelings prepared for your arrival. The rest was up to you.

Although you have now returned home, Gelnoff will always be with you. Keep these rings in a safe place, not only as a keepsake to your adventures in Gelnoff, but as your gateway to return to the village should you need to.

Your father and I love you to the ends of the earth and back. Stay close and look out for each other.

Mom

Two keys were placed inside the envelope along with a note which explained how the gold key unlocked a safe deposit box full of cash and the silver one led them home. Camryn slipped both keys into her pocket and refolded the letter.

As she stuffed the letter in her back pocket, a Canadian Eskimo puppy with a scar over his left eye peeked out from behind the rock.

"Camryn, look. There's a puppy over there." Toby encouraged the pup to come closer. "Come here, boy."

The puppy ran to him and licked his face.

Toby looked the puppy in the eye and knew right away this puppy was the dire wolf. Tears of joy streamed down his face. "I thought you were dead. How did you get here?"

A gravelly voice behind him explained, "The Treelings used the restoring power of Water to revive him."

Toby turned around, and a giant Minotaur towered over him. "Noraz!"

The Minotaur grinned. "The pup's name is Phelon. He is my gift to you."

Toby rose to his feet and ran to greet Noraz. "Thank you."

"No, thank you, Guardian, for returning my children to me. Because of you, my family is home safely. The Treelings have returned to Alderwood, clans have reclaimed their land and rebuilt villages, and the elements have reunited. Balance has been restored, and you have brought peace and harmony back to Gelnoff. We are eternally grateful." He bowed respectfully.

"How did you get here?"

He opened his fist to reveal a bright yellow gemstone. "The Air stone transported me here. Its power is limited, however, and I must return soon."

"We'll miss you," Camryn said, giving Noraz a hug.

"And I you. But you must return to your life, and I must return to mine. Both of you will forever be in my heart, though, and I will never forget you."

He released Camryn and cleared his throat, and for a moment Camryn thought she saw him wipe tears from his eyes.

"I must go," Noraz said. "Take care, you two. And remember, the rings can always lead you back to Gelnoff."

"Thank you, Noraz, for everything."

"So long, children, and godspeed." Noraz waved goodbye then vanished in a wisp of yellow light.

Almost simultaneously, a shiny blue car appeared in the middle of the road. "Where did that come from?" Toby asked.

"I have no idea." Camryn pulled the silver key from her pocket and stared at it. "But I have a feeling I know what this key is for. Let's go home," she said.

Toby couldn't have agreed more. "Please."

Toby, Camryn, and Phelon made their way to the car and climbed inside. Camryn took the wheel and slid the silver key into the ignition. The engine revved and the dashboard lit up, revealing a full tank of gas. The puppy poked his head out the window while Camryn and Toby buckled their seatbelts. When everyone was secure, Camryn put the car in drive, placed her foot on the gas pedal, and steered them toward home.

The End

About the Author

When not writing, L.M. Nelson is a certified teacher and CPR/First Aid instructor. She enjoys poetry, gardening, music, and photography. You can often find her outside on wilderness walks soaking in the beauty of nature. The Guardian is her fifth novel.

Aside from her novels, she has written several poems, some of which have been selected for literary magazines and published in poetry collections. She co-wrote the article, 'Gifted and Talented Education at the Close of the Decade of the Brain', which was published in an Idaho educational journal, and has contributed articles to various blogs.

L.M. Nelson grew up in California and the Pacific Northwest, but currently resides in South Central Texas with her husband and two children. You can visit her website at lmnelsonscorner.wordpress.com or follow her on Facebook, Twitter, or Instagram.

Other novels by L.M. Nelson
Scrubs
Sand & Sutures
Beyond the Hardwood
Center Stage